T0196630

# Damn the Novel

When a Privileged Genre Prevails Over
All Forms of Creative Writing

AMR MUNEER DAHAB

Translated from Arabic by Youssef Elharrak
Translation reviewed by Amr Muneer Dahab

authorHOUSE®

*AuthorHouse*™
*1663 Liberty Drive*
*Bloomington, IN 47403*
*www.authorhouse.com*
*Phone: 1 (800) 839-8640*

© *2019 Amr Muneer Dahab. All rights reserved.*

*No part of this book may be reproduced, stored in a retrieval system, or transmitted by any means without the written permission of the author.*

*Published by AuthorHouse 07/23/2019*

*ISBN: 978-1-5462-7132-1 (sc)*
*ISBN: 978-1-5462-7130-7 (hc)*
*ISBN: 978-1-5462-7131-4 (e)*

*Library of Congress Control Number: 2018914481*

*Print information available on the last page.*

*Any people depicted in stock imagery provided by Getty Images are models, and such images are being used for illustrative purposes only. Certain stock imagery © Getty Images.*

*This book is printed on acid-free paper.*

*Because of the dynamic nature of the Internet, any web addresses or links contained in this book may have changed since publication and may no longer be valid. The views expressed in this work are solely those of the author and do not necessarily reflect the views of the publisher, and the publisher hereby disclaims any responsibility for them.*

To Muneer Muhammad Dahab, for being a ROLE MODEL

# Contents

# WHY THIS BOOK NOW?

This book, as its subtitle suggests, is about supremacy among the different forms of creative writing. It is, above all, a condemnation of those who deploy their impact on the concerned public opinion (mainly consisting of readers and critics) to advocate a privilege to be granted to a genre so that it can take over the rest of the existing literary genres. Worst of all, the backers of this perspective argue that "the granted privilege" is an ineluctable fate equivalent to the *historical imperatives* in politics and economy.

This book might be received as an ungrounded, vociferous cry against the novel per se, but it is not. It is simply against perpetuating the delusion that the novel is inevitably the most dominating and influential literary genre of the time. Let's suppose that the supremacy of lyrical poetry over all other forms of Arabic creative writing throughout the different periods of the Arabic literary tradition was really an error that did much harm to Arabic literature. The very same error is being reproduced by crowning the novel as the leading genre capable of taking over not only the interest of the reading public, but also the dedication of the critics.

It is time for Arabic literature to start anew by giving all genres the same chance to flourish in total freedom without any sort of secret or manifest "patronage."

*Damn the Novel* deplores all plans by devotees to make the creative writing form they cherish the most prominent and predominant, as if they possessed the (Holy) Divine Delegation to mute the voices of all other existing genres.

Furthermore, although I possess my own objective reasons to stand on the opposite side of the novel's camp, I would like to express my

1

delight that, having waged this war against the novel, it has never succeeded in driving me to its shores of seduction, nor has it managed to trap me in the snares of its love.

**Amr**
**April 18, 2017**

# Damn the Novel!

Whenever I propose one of my book drafts to a publisher, believing that I am making an appealing offer, his response always takes the same form: "We'd rather see a novel!" In a similar vein, an esteemed publisher responded jokingly, but somehow seriously, to my perpetual expression of avoidance of every potential esteem or affection for the novel: "What about writing a novel against novels?" Gaber Asfour,[1] the renowned Egyptian literary critic, has incessantly articulated that "we are living in the novel's era." The slogan, having survived for many years now, is still spontaneously uttered every now and then within literary circles. But Asfour has ushered in a new dictum that defines the modern time according to a literary perspective similar to the existing dicta, including the Era of the Internet and the Era of Speed.

If the Era of the Novel were not an expression of underestimation toward the other literary genres, I would take the lead in supporting a definition of our time anchored in literature. It would be honoring a craft that has been subject to much unfairness. In fact, literature has been resisting marginalization so audaciously that it merits homage for staying alive.

But the slogan is designed to tease poetry rather than the Internet or speed. The more the dictum in question is being propagated, the more conscious we become of the fact that poetry, in spite of topping the list of presumed enemies, is not the only target. The list also includes the short story, which has ultimately been designated as the novel's

---

[1] Gaber Asfour has been an Egyptian professor at Cairo University since 1966. He was appointed Egypt's Minister of Culture on February 1, 2011. He has published *Countering Fanaticism*, *Times of the Novel*, and *In Defense of the Enlightenment*, among others.

fiercest opponent in the race to leadership, given that poetry has already been kicked out of the game. Short prose narrative, basically the short story, remains a potential rival supported by a handful of writers—the majority of whom would strive to acquire the prestigious title of "novelist" rather than being referred to as, simply, "short story writers."

Because the transition from short story writing to novel writing requires no more than the acquisition of (some) additional knowledge and little expertise to keep up with the rhythm of a longer race, it was not that tough for those prose writers who opted to begin the journey. Worse still, many poets, said to have been custodians of the Arabic poetic tradition, have been captivated by the new wave—that is, the novel—that has sprung from a Western background and not from any of the forms of Arabic prose that have existed since the pre-Islamic era (*Jahiliyyah*).[2]

Literature is said to be a contagious temptation leading to new shores of experimentation and unique expectation. Nevertheless, mobility within literary genres seems to predominantly be a show, rather than an honest devotion to any sort of wordsmithing arts. There is no harm, as far as I am concerned, in the pursuit of the craft during a writer's innocently naïve intellectual adolescence, nor is there any shame voyaging across the different fields of creative writing as an example of the author's prowess and to show off, provided it is possible to master more than one literary genre. Accordingly, any obsession with shifting from one genre to another only for the sake of being awarded titles (of honor) has nothing to do with the process of stepping patiently across the long, bumpy path of writing in different genres, regardless of the success or failure it may ultimately reap.

And so, there is no doubt that those who curse the novel are not always writers whom the long narrative genre has never been able to seduce. There exist many other sects of literary professionals along with numerous eager followers who have declared a similar stand. Most poets and poetry devotees are said to show much more bitterness in this respect. In different words, they are the biggest losers in this "Era

---

[2] *Jahiliyyah* (Arabic: جَاهِلِيَّة *ğāhiliyyah/jāhilīyah* "ignorance") is an Islamic concept of the period of time and state of affairs in Arabia before the advent of Islam. It is often translated as the "Age of Ignorance."

of the Novel," because poetry has always been, throughout the history of Arabic literature, regarded as the most superior genre, worthy of domination over all other genres.

However, the short story is another big loser, in the sense that it was close to being crowned the leading literary genre before it was bitterly disqualified from the race to the peak. The readers eventually decided, in this Era of Speed, to side with the "long-distance race."

Novelists, as well as the novel's devotees, are to cheer their presumed victory as they like, but they should do it without prompting us to share their "inevitable" perspective on the basis of a deceptive conceptualization or, as we have just seen, on reverse logic (i.e., the decision to side with the long-distance race in the Era of Speed).

# Coming Late Across Tayeb Salih

Twenty years or more ago, when I was a young man, driven by fondness for Arabic classical verse—to the extent of believing it to be the one and only literary genre worthy of reading and writing, rather than by apparent sensitiveness about novels—I used to see in Tayeb Salih[3] merely that outstanding Sudanese literary figure who should have been a poet, not a novelist.

After I broke up with poetry in a smoothly refined manner, I did not seek to engage myself in any form of the arts of fiction. Thus, my "allergy" to the novel, the prevailing trend of the time, has never faded. Shifting away from the shores of verse, the novel has never been a choice, since I opted for essay writing as an alternative destination. Similarly, I continue to view Salih as someone who merits deep esteem for his notoriety both in the Arabic region and all over the world—not merely for his novelistic charm.

It is surprising that my praise for the man's particularity and genius, which I came across late, was not based on his peculiar talent as an essayist. It was not his columns that could bridge the gap between me and his novels; but, unexpectedly, it was his very novelistic repertoire, and precisely his most known piece of all his work, *Season of Migration to the North*,[4] that led me to his fiction.

---

[3] Tayeb Salih is one of the best known Arabic novelists of the twentieth century. His 1966 masterpiece *Season of Migration to the North*—voted one of the 100 best works of fiction in 2002—was declared to be the most important Arabic novel of the twentieth century by the Arab Literary Academy in 2001.

[4] A classic postcolonial Sudanese novel published in Arabic in 1966, *Season of Migration to the North* has since been translated into more than twenty languages. The English translation was published in 1969 as part of the influential Heinemann African Writers Series. It was described by Edward Said as one of the six great novels in Arabic literature.

Honestly, what attracted me to this unique novel was not merely its style, or what some described as a land where prose and verse coexist, but rather the way the web of its narrative structure was constructed. In this sense, what I liked the most in *Season of Migration*, the phenomenal fiction, was the very narrative phase. This fantastically built piece of work should be regarded, at least by me being a Sudanese citizen, as more than mere exceptional workmanship. It is thanks to *Season of Migration* that the Sudanese novelist is significantly renowned worldwide. Most masterpieces have purely artistic strengths worthy of esteem and admiration. In the same vein, unique and new styles can constitute a supplementary reason, even for those who are not used to the conventional style in novels, to read, or even become addicted to, fiction. Additionally, the bold idea and the audacious approach are two other creative ingredients rendering *Season of Migration*, along with its author, worthy of appreciation and estimation.

By the same token, I kept the same inverted logic that governs my outlook on literary genres when it came to Tayeb Salih, whose essays appeared to me as worthy of affection, though their charm seemed to have been simmered on a low heat—a charm not besieged by an aura of majesty like that characterizing the novelistic genre. Salih's articles have earned well-deserved recognition for their simplicity, rather than their grandeur—which is especially important given the recession and poor reputation of the product in question (the essay) within the field of creative writing.

Tayeb Salih the essayist, at least as far as I am concerned, is not inferior to Tayeb Salih the novelist; however, there still exist numerous prominent critics (not only devoted literary lovers) who are entangled in a reading process obsessed with a hierarchical point of view. On this basis, they are always concerned with listing literary genres according to an ordinal order they advocate, and not according to a categorization that approaches literary pieces of work, or any other creative form, based on their merit, regardless of the genre they belong to.

Tayeb Salih is an eminent columnist who realized from the very start that essay writing is an independent creative practice that is not, by any means, inferior to novel writing. Thus, being inhabited by the same passion of an artist eager for inspiration, he would get immersed in a writing experience that incorporated the two genres on an equal footing. He used to receive questions like, "Why did you quit writing?" He would answer, "I still write articles in newspapers, magazines, and books." His response is, of course, disappointing, or even provocative, for those who are fond of the idol that tops the proclaimed literary hierarchy.

However, the great writer, who's great because of his feel for art and life and not because he's achieved status after the publication of a novel or two, has always been conscious of his primary mission: spreading the wings of his creativity, whatever his literary garment (a novel, a short story, or an article). As for classical poetry—one of Salih's devotions— the man did not take the risk of defying the complications of rhyme and rhythm. He simply chose to deal with verse as a connoisseur, not more. Furthermore, being deeply honest with himself and with others, he even ceased to write novels, the raison d'être of his triumphant writing experience, once he felt that his words were created spontaneously as essays.

Accordingly, I would say, without exaggeration, that Tayeb Salih always treated life as multiple instances of creativity manifested in every possible way. Thus, most of the man's intimate meetings, attended by friends and passersby alike, were a fountain of unprompted innovation— an original process of creation independent from (and not inferior to) both novel and essay writing, though being unmanageable when it comes to putting them into written (creative) texts.

# "Damn the Novel!"

## Thus Tayeb Salih Himself Might Have Protested

I can hardly name any critic who has dealt with Tayeb Salih without referring to the man's scarce novelistic output or even accusing him of leading a barren phase of his life as a novelist shortly after *Season of Migration*. On the other hand, as we stated elsewhere, Alaa Al-Aswany[5] has pointed out that scarcity is the rule when it comes to novelists (though I do not believe this applies to Al-Aswany), with the exception of Naguib Mahfouz[6] and a few others worldwide.

Nonetheless, whether "novelistic scarcity" is the rule or the exception, creativity should be measured in terms of quality (how?), even when referring to one piece of work, rather than in terms of quantity (how many?). In this very context, though not being his only novel, *Season of Migration* is said to be a good illustration of how Salih could figure prominently in the Arab as well as in the global literary scene despite the fact that his critics kept awaiting a new tour de force equivalent to his previous masterpiece. They wanted concrete evidence to prove the man's talent, and they received, in return, an embarrassing question: "What if I don't write any more books?" The response arose

---

[5] Born May 27, 1957, in Cairo, Egypt, Egyptian author Al-Aswany is known for his bestselling novels and his vocal criticism of Egyptian president Hosni Mubarak. Aswany's first major novel, *'Imārat Yaʿqūbiyyān* (*The Yacoubian Building*), attracted an unprecedented number of readers in Egypt and throughout the Arab world when it was published in 2002.

[6] Naguib Mahfouz (1911–2006) was an Egyptian novelist and screenwriter who was awarded the Nobel Prize for Literature in 1988, the first Arabic writer to be so honored.

of its own accord: "It doesn't matter. One novel is enough." In fact, Arab critics seemed to be the most obsessed with both the question and answer above, whereas great writers from all over the globe have always been valued by the uniqueness of a particular novel, rather than the number of titles listed in a writer's resume.

I think Tayeb Salih was not the kind of writer to count exclusively on the greatness of one novel in lieu of writing successive pieces of work for the sake of some other instances of unique creativity. Alternatively, he insisted that he should keep himself away from (or even break up for good with) long fiction in order to embrace new horizons above "genre borders." Short story writing was only an option, among other creative genres, coexisting with his (seemingly native) devotion to essay writing.

In spite of the truth about the smoothness of his novels and short stories alike, namely his masterpiece *Season of Migration to the North*, Tayeb Salih's primary obsession consisted of, above all, his writing experience as an essayist. His essays were always the fruit of a sincere and deliberate inspiration free from the reins of any hasty assignment that would pay based on the number of words printed on columns limited in space. These essays were extensive in the eyes of readers and critics who evaluated his essays not by any drastic standards. However, Salih seems to have committed himself to essay writing being driven by the same respect he granted to his novelistic experience. The only harm that the man's articles could have done is that they were provocative in the sense that they ruled out any possibility of a potential new novel capable of quenching the thirst of those eager devotees (believing in the novel for the novel's sake).

What made Tayeb Salih an exceptional essayist was not only his encyclopedic knowledge as a well-read person who knew how to deploy the privilege of mastering both Arabic and English, but also his outlook on the essay as a majestic literary genre—not as a profitable routine that (might) help cover some of the basic expenses.

It is very unlikely that novelists can write exceptionally great essays if they arrogantly descend from their (novel) ivory tower believing in the simplicity of essay writing, whose supposed easy structure is perceived as rather an accessible genre unworthy of respect. Similarly, the novel knows well how to reinforce the same shortsightedness so as to trap dedicated readers (victims) into its snare.

Before being an honest writer, Tayeb Salih was an honest man. He ceased writing novels once he felt he had nothing new to tell through that literary genre; he never avoided being an essayist merely for fear of risking his reputable image as a novelist—losing the prestigious title by its being combined with, or replaced by, "essayist," "columnist," or, barely, "writer."

Tayeb Salih ceases to write when he doesn't have anything to say. Taking into account the man's simple temperament, it does make sense when he sometimes resorts to silence despite having something to articulate. This is either because the events are worthy of much more than the usual approach or because the context does not allow the needed level of candor, whatever the form of expression.

Many critics would prefer if a number of writers could avoid producing pieces of work that were closer to redundancy than to creativity. Naguib Mahfouz was absolutely not among this category of writers. The Moroccan critic Said Yaktine smartly pointed out that the Nobel Prize holder was subject to a great deal of influence from Arab novelists throughout the eighties and seventies. This is a manifest illustration of Mahfouz's intelligence and flexibility, which he should be credited for.

Compared to Mahfouz, Tayeb Salih did not only refuse to be affected by the mood created by the younger generation of novelists coming after him, he even did not let himself repeat the same novelistic experience he had once ushered in. Instead, he preferred to try something different or even cease writing for a while. It seems as if Naguib Mahfouz (according to the same comparison between the two great writers made by Yaktine) could not afford any good excuse or plan to dispose of fiction writing basically because he used to master/cherish nothing more than narrative prose among all forms of creative writing. This, on the other hand, might sometimes help writers multiply their output—multiplicity not as a defect per se, provided it is being done with care and expertise—and accordingly establish their independent approach to literature and art (creativity) in general.

If Tayeb Salih were not that well-mannered person armed with an economy of speech along with an unconditional devotion to and esteem for writing, I wouldn't hesitate to imagine him turning on his heels were a narrative fiction devotee to inquire about the upcoming novel. He alternatively resorts to either a complete desertion of writing or an embrace of the elegant perspectives of essay writing. "Damn the novel!" he would cry out.

# A Cease-fire

Dealing with a unique novel like *Season of Migration to the North* or an exceptional short story writer like the Nubian (Egyptian) Haggag Hassan Oddoul,[7] I find myself obliged to cease my feelings of enmity toward narrative fiction (that is, the novel) as a sign of my goodwill. I might say that my aversion to the literary genres in question is a spontaneous act free of any kind of deliberate malice.

Experts in the different branches of psychology and social conduct, as well as preachers from every part of the globe, warn us against expressing our judgments based on prior impressions (and/or stereotypes) whose delight is irresistible most of the time. However, I think there is no harm in having prior impressions provided they are not meant to be a form of criticism in regard to people and their creative output.

However, my position toward the novel is much more than a mere prior impression. It comes from a journey that started at poetry as my first love. Later on, the journey expanded to include other (written and not written) forms of creativity, but with a bias toward the essay, even at the expense of poetry. Nevertheless, my literary taste can veer toward novels and short stories as long as they are creatively well constructed. Here lies the difference between devotees of a category of creative writing and those who have already taken a stand in regard to a literary genre. The first group of readers is open to all possibilities of various levels of creativity responding to their (literary) appetite. The second group keeps awaiting only good and perhaps exceptional pieces of work.

---

[7] Haggag Hassan Oddoul (born in 1944 in Alexandria, Egypt) is an Egyptian writer of Nubian descent, and a campaigner for the rights of the Nubian people. He is basically famous for his *Nights of Musk*.

In this context, there seems to be no difference between the attitude of those who like only delicious food and the position of those who like exclusively "attractive" pieces of art. One who says he likes oranges only if they are medium-sized, colorful, and juicy is automatically setting conditions for his love. The opposite, of course, is when someone loves something, let's say oranges, without imposing a list of conditions.

Because it is difficult to resist the stench of stardom, the novel (the star of this time in regard to the number of fans) does not cease seducing even its most dedicated opponents until it unmercifully defeats them. These opponents may sometimes conceal their defeat, but they cannot resist following the echoes of a prevailing literary genre.

*The Longing of the Dervish* is a novel by the Sudanese novelist Hammour Ziada[8] that has made me, once more, seek some shade (and peace) under the tree of a novel I haven't read yet. All I have read are some pieces of news concerning the novel winning a prestigious prize and being on the shortlist of an important Arab award. My stay in the novel's shade has been reinforced at the sight of the fifth edition of the book in question occupying a space in every possible bookshop with the resounding notation on the cover: THIS NOVEL IS ON THE SHORTLIST OF THE BOOKER PRIZE. As an adversary of the new trend of awards (especially novel prizes), I should have gotten furious, but I unexpectedly wanted more peace and shade.

Furthermore, it seems that *The Longing of the Dervish* has attracted me thanks to its ability to create a (novelistic) phenomenon: I haven't had the chance to behold its charm simply because I haven't read it so far. The attraction to the said phenomenon consists, first of all, in the potency of a sort of creative writing (I don't like much) to captivate the concern of a large part of the public, especially in a context in which reading has become such a rare routine. Second, it is amazing that the novel (reinforced by the magical influence of the prize itself) is able to

---

[8] Hammour Ziada (born 1979) is a Sudanese writer and journalist. He has worked as a civil society and human rights researcher and is currently a journalist based in Cairo. He is best known for his second novel *The Longing of the Dervish* (2014), which won the Naguib Mahfouz Prize in 2014 and was also nominated for the 2015 Arabic Booker Prize.

highlight the dark/marginalized corners of the Arab culture so as to make them breathe a fresh new air—an almost impossible mission.

My truce in this sense is not merely a reconsideration of my prior impressions vis-à-vis the novel, but primarily a matter of deserved gratitude toward a literary genre that hasn't managed to gain my attention. The said authority of the novelistic phenomenon might magically manifest its influence in spite of our stubborn intention to escape the shores of seduction.

# Thermometer of Writing

The UAE Writers Union invited me to give a lecture in Abu Dhabi. I seized the opportunity to tackle an issue that I entitled "The Thermometer of Serious Creative Writing." Later, I decided to omit the word "serious" from the title because I thought that identifying the standards of serious writing means that the opposite standards are automatically those of nonserious writing, without the need to mention them.

In fact, to approach a topic with no existing methodological definition is both difficult and easy at the same time. On the one hand, it is hard because you have to establish a methodological identification and approach, but on the other hand, it is easy because your new definition will have no existing alternative, although it might be an easy target for critics' skirmishes in the future.

Juggling between the two ideas, the thought asserted itself till it became clear in my mind. All the ingredients for the conference were there and all I needed, in two days, was a close revision of the themes of the imminent debate.

The interventions of the audience along with a brief overview of four culture sections in the Emirati daily newspapers reveal that, in spite of the seductive enthusiasm for the adventure, no matter how clear and precise the language of the debater is, one conference can never be enough to handle such a controversial issue overnight.

It is more likely that the challenge of promoting a new concept lies not in the ability of its promoter to analyze and simplify it but, most importantly, in responding to the questions of every eager intervener, especially if the questions and insights look strange or unexpected. There is no guarantee that your audience shall accept your proofs simply because you believe in your cause. They may, and have the right to, view the matter from different angles. They won't just submissively listen to you while highlighting your "presumed discovery," as you may have imagined.

The lecture centered on introducing the concepts of "serious writing" and "light writing" as commonly referenced by both critics and the public. My objective was to get to the fact that there exist no accurate definitions of any of the two concepts. There is only that general impression that grants appreciation and consideration to "serious writing." "Light writing," on the contrary, is commonly seen as not worthy of much esteem, or even as a disrespectful aspect of creativeness.

"Serious writing" is commonly said to take the shape of pieces of writing comparatively greater in terms of word and page count and to primarily tend to appear more rigorous than satirical (though it has been realized that irony/ satire is not often the opposite of seriousness), ushering in the birth of a new idea (this is one signal of seriousness that we will not disagree about, as we will see shortly).

However, there are some common signs within "light writing" models themselves that help reinforce their negative evaluation and acquisition—namely, limited number of words and pages; easy access to the meaning of the subject matter, even if they might bring some new thoughts or address an existing problematic issue in a revolutionary way; and an ironical style, even when expressed with a great deal of originality.

The primary concern of my approach, ever since I was taken over by the issue and its dimensions, focuses on highlighting the discrepancy between "light writing" and "junk writing" (or even worthless writing). There are many examples of "light writing" that incorporate interesting and influential contents, whereas there exist a number of pieces of writing said to be "serious" that, apart from the desire for a "respectful" outcome, bring nothing new in terms of thought or style.

For this reason, I took the initiative of proposing a third category termed "junk writing" or "worthless writing." I did not see any harm in describing this category of writing as absurd in both form and meaning. Some of the attendees expressed their reservation that any writing should be described as absurd. Despite my certainty about the existence of such a category of writing (which historically has fallen under the title of "light writing"), I do not mind referring to "worthless writing," especially when it tends to embrace vulgarity, as fallacious rather than silly, like a number of the attendees suggested. Although creating a new term is not my central preoccupation in this respect, "weak" is the most suitable term to stand for "unworthy" forms of "light writing." In fact, people are still in need of a term capable of venting their condemnation vis-à-vis pieces of (creative) work forged with a great deal of noticeably bad faith. In this context, they won't hesitate to describe them as "trivial" or even "disrespectful." Some of the attendants pointed out that an expression such as "trivial writing" cannot be considered a critical term. In turn, I noted that "serious writing" and "light writing" are also not critical terms, though both of them are deployed by critics when it comes to the general assessment of a given piece of work or writer.

To clarify the signification of the above terminology, the existing ones along with the ones I intend to introduce, the subject matter can be summed up as follows: "Serious writing" is a process of bringing about some new thought contributing to (human) knowledge either through the creation of an original idea or via the analysis of an already existing concept. This type of writing does not necessarily seek to please its readers, nor does it care much about the number of words or pages. "Light writing," on the other hand, is often short and is obsessed with pleasing its audience. It may offer fresh content if not merely explaining or commenting on other (serious or light) works. The third category, "weak writing," is an unworthy/ineffective sort of writing that may acquire the attributes of vulgarity. It brings nothing new and ranges from limited to high word counts. However, it is mainly concerned with being interesting though superficial (not simple, for simplicity can never constitute a weakness in writing). In addition, it often tends to tickle the public responding to their desired expectations rather than exposing them to the challenging taboos.

Dispute is likely to take place—in every possible way—because we tend to use the same words but refer to distinct, or even contradictory, meanings.

# Anyone Can Write a Novel

"The common direction along the pathway of literature leads generally from poetry to prose and not the other way around; we rarely—I say 'rarely' though I would rather say we never—find any writer who started his literary life as a storyteller or as an essayist and then, later on when his (poetic) talent suddenly flourished, at an old age, convert to poetry. Al-Nabigha Al-Dhubiani,[9] whose poetic genius showed up comparatively at the autumn of his life, himself did not dare to write short stories in the manner Chekhov did before shifting to verse that deserved the honor of being hung on the walls of the Kaaba as a Mu'allaqa.[10] Instead, he started as a poet who might have postponed the announcement of his poetic zeal in public. . . ."

In one of my books, *O Writers, Be Humble* (from which the above paragraph is extracted), though it was not my intention to deal with Al-Dhubiani as a poetic phenomenon, I think it is worth referring to what I pointed out there in this context. If Al-Dhubiani had decided to write prose, he would have fell short of attracting a number of dedicated critics and devotees alike. On the contrary, he could not escape the authority of verse, which was more influential, from the seductive power of prose. The temptations of a potential reverse migration to the

---

[9] Al-Nabigha Al-Dhubiani was one of the last Arabian poets of pre-Islamic times. "Al-Nabigha" means "genius" in Arabic. He is one of the six eminent pre-Islamic poets whose poems were collected before the middle of the second century of Islam, and have been regarded as the standard of Arabic poetry. These poets wrote long poems comparable to epic poems.

[10] The Mu'allaqāt is a group of seven long Arabic poems that are considered the best work of the pre-Islamic era. The name means The Suspended Odes or The Hanging Poems, the traditional explanation being that these poems were hung on or in the Kaaba at Mecca.

opposite shore of creativity were too weak to make him, along with his fellow poets, desert a creative craftsmanship able to bring money and fame in exchange for a poor art that would bring none of the sought privileges.

The power of poetry sustained for more than a thousand years in the lives of Arabs until the sedition of the novel took over contemporary Arabic literature, encouraging a large number of Arab writers to launch their presumably promising and prosperous novelistic projects. Furthermore, some of them already opted, without any prior notice, for a migration from poetry, or other literary genres, to the bosom of the new trend: the novel.

To continue from *O Writers, Be Humble:* "The direction along the pathway of literature (that almost every writer tries writing poetry at the beginning of his writing experience) is the strongest evidence that poetry holds a temptation over every writer. I believe even those who were not known for their attempts to compose verse used to conceal their pages, maybe wisely, when they realized that they were not born to write according to rhythm and rhyme, but rather to use words consistent with their semantic limits." However, as we saw in the previous paragraph, the situation has turned upside down, and signs of radical change have multiplied so fast, that we come to see young beginners, or those who have converted to the new trend only lately, with minor talent, insist on publishing their work or even persistently submitting their novels to be considered for prestigious literary awards.

It should not be understood that what I said above is another way to condemn those writers, being young or elderly, whose novels deserve esteem and awards for their work per se. Instead, I suggest that novel writing is distinct from composing poetry, in the sense that poetry, as a poet put it, "is as hard as a long journey." On the contrary, it seems that the mission of a novelist is not so tough that even a starter can realize miraculous achievement to be honored by the most prominent prizes on the first or second attempt. Similarly, an old man can, all of a sudden, discover his novelistic (exceptional!) gift worthy of glory, prominent awards, and honorable titles.

Let's proceed with the same poetic insight attributed to

Al-Hutay'ah,[11] who wisely pointed out that poetry is a journey "if taken by the ignorant/his steps will end up in the abyss." Whoever defies poetry and its sound masters believing he is so superior as to deserve a higher position among the existing poets will ultimately fall to the worst destination. The word "abyss" in the verse above includes every possible instance of humiliation and decay.

On the contrary, the Arabic novel has been very merciful, in terms of the expenses of the journey and the consequences of failure, to those who dared experiencing narrative fiction. Weak novels, as long as they are spiced with excitement, can easily be welcomed by publishers and sit on the shelves of libraries, in spite of their modest aesthetic value. Bad poetry, on the other hand, is automatically condemned by everyone to the extent that no publisher would look at it (Arab publishers are already unwilling to publish even those collections of poems considered original), let alone accusing it of belonging to something else—but not to poetry.

Considering Al-Hutay'ah's radical stand in regard to the art of verse along with the enthusiastic conduct of the advocates of a trend abounding with prestigious awards, I think that any evaluation/ assessment of literary genres should not be obsessed with measuring the length of the mission along the pathway of writing or the potential hardships and disastrous consequences of an uncalculated journey. What really matters is the ongoing impression of a work when the temporary fever of the trend dies out. In this respect, for centuries poetry has had a magically concrete effect on Arabs, while the Arabic novelistic experience still has a very long way to traverse before history should prove the possibility of such an achievement.

---

[11] Jarwal Ibn Aws al-Hutay'ah (died 650–668 C.E.) was from the al-Hijaz region of Saudi Arabia. His poetry was largely satirical and his style was influenced by medieval Arabic poetry.

21

# Liars!

Poetry is said to be governed by this dictum: "The more lies it tells, the more beauty it brings about." The novel goes far beyond this old adage about verse; I wouldn't be exaggerating if I said that it is the biggest lie in contemporary Arabic literature. If "poetic lies" stand for basically the remote perspectives to which the poet's wild imagination may lead, the novel deserves the title of "the biggest lie" as it is, above all, an instance of fantasy whose credibility is doubtful in spite of the novelist's seemingly honest claim that their work is based on a real story. A piece of literary work is not regarded by critics as worthy of being a "real novel" if it just mimics life without embracing the boundless horizons of imagination. Similarly, readers seek novels that fly across the perspectives of fantasy before they're seen as worthy of support and devotion.

The above-mentioned imagination is only an act of deviation away from reality (truth?) that goes beyond just changing the names of places and heroes—or their roles in the novel—to inventing a course of events, along with narrative knots that lead to multiple presumed endings, none of which necessarily correspond to the real story the whole work is based on. Is there a more flagrant evidence of mendacity in creative writing than this?

Al-Asma'i[12] is famous for his saying, "Poetry is a house of misery whose gate is evil, so if it seeks the good it turns weak." Similarly, the novel would have been described accordingly if it had survived the brilliant Arab critic more than a thousand years ago. In fact, Al-Asma'i's

---

[12] Al-Asma'i (c. 740–828 C.E.) was one of the earliest Arabic lexicographers and one of the three leaders of the Basra school of Arabic grammar. He was also a pioneer of natural science and zoology.

dictum, in addition to the concept that "the more lies poetry tells, the more beauty it brings about," applies to all other genres of literature and art, not only poetry (like it was said more than ten centuries ago as a veneration of its artistic value) and the novel (having no intention to venerate narrative fiction in this context). Both statements are intended only to emphasize the fact that moral values are narrowing down perspectives for any literary and artistic aesthetics to the extent that the two (morality and beauty) often seem to be at odds with each other.

By the same token, the temptation of the novel is not less potent than the seduction of verse, no matter how different the interpretations of this Quranic verse: "As for those poets, only the perverse follow them."[13] We have just seen how novelists subject reality (and the truth being the opposite of fiction) to overt fabrications more than poets do when it comes to "telling lies" throughout literary work as a transgression of reality away from any trials about morality. Novelists are, therefore, more willing to go too far in every direction and say things that they cannot do. Worst of all, even their "job description" is grounded mainly on that sort of wandering and deliberate transcendence not only of "things they cannot do" but also of the challenging, or potentially impossible, attempts of the community (or any social context) across the pathway of knowledge and truth assimilation.

Accordingly, novelists are excellent liars. They have committed more lies than those told by poets—their poor colleagues who have been violently criticized for a sin they did not commit. All they did was let their imagination accelerate in a light way that did no harm to reality. While poets would set their imagination free to fly to faraway destinations (not always innocently but with a great deal of economy and respect vis-à-vis the different literary worlds), novelists have broken into those worlds not through their widest gates but across the doors of falsity, basically to weave their own worlds that have already taken over the hearts of beholders among distinguished critics and the general public in a way that calls for boredom. Poets felt the huge threat dragging the red carpet from beneath their feet after they had been walking proudly under the lights of public literary prominence for centuries. This is perhaps a reason why it is believed that the biggest

---

[13] The Holy Quran (Ash-Shu'ara/The Poets 26:224–26).

losers in this context are generally poets, many of whom have rushed to walk in the steps of the new trend and its prestigious prizes; I, among others, do have my reasons for strongly protesting against any new "fad" in life when it diverges away from its original creativity to turn into apparently an "individual obligation."

Thus is the authority of "new trends," either related to the way we use clothing to beautify our bodies or the way we create pieces of literature and art to feed our souls. This is regardless of the truth claimed by each party in literature and art (and life as a whole) in a nonstop process of inventing sweet lies.

# Excessive Rhetoric of Fantasy

It is still hard to overcome the problematic matter of judging literature with reference to ethics, which is already a deep issue in our (Arab) societies. But the notion about "telling lies" as suggested in the dictum of "the more lies poetry tells, the more beauty it brings about" has always been palatable in Arabic societies regarding poetic lies as instances of rhetoric exaggeration whereby Arabic lyric poetry—throughout the centuries before the modern era—tended to access far horizons of unlimited imagination. The repertoire of Arabic poetry is full of many rhetorical images that were merely exaggerations woven with much skill and beauty so as to perform their poetic ends (praise, pride, lamentation, satire, romantic love, and so on).

When it comes to the novel, supporters of sending literature to ethical trials—fierce opponents of "poetry lies" regardless of their "aesthetic sweetness"—are in real trouble, except for those who persist in rejecting the "new trend" (the novel) as a whole for being the offspring of a big lie— as we saw in the previous essay—while verse contents itself with "light lies" capable of affording charm without distorting truth. However, the novel, unlike poetry, did not accept the ambiguous stand of the "intransigent" lovers of literature who are obsessed with morality judgment. Despite the dominance of news stories about banned novels for religious, ethical, social, or political reasons, we haven't heard about any famous slogan condemning the novel (which is purely a fabric of fantasy/lies) in principle.

That was the novel's deserved victory. It is, of course, not our objective here to ignite the fire of sedition that leads to questioning the eligibility of this modern literary art (especially to the Arabs) to be granted absolute welcome in principle, although one of the most important purposes of this approach is to deplore people's submission to the novel such that it has almost exclusively taken over their literary tastes.

The controversy of "the ethically stubborn opponents" of the novel has been, in this respect, obsessed with the thematic messages being transmitted via the new trend's central idea or those infiltrating through its outlets of style and artistic imagery. The controversy has not been focused on the charm grounded in lies/fantasy/exaggeration, as was the case with Arabic lyric poetry in ancient times.

The novel deserves praise to the extent that it excels in weaving a wonderful lie that readers accept for granted, believing in its inevitability. Worst of all, pleasure and interest are said to be acquired exclusively through the perspective of that exquisite lie.

If extravagance is generally blameworthy on every level, the novel being not an exception, extravagance in terms of imagination is not a defect in itself in the novel unless it tends to turn superlatively excessive. Moreover, novelistic unbounded imagination is honored and distinguished to the extent that a new piece of vocabulary is introduced: "fantasy," which can include other literary and creative forms. Our lyric poetry is said to be a "nonfantastic art" whose lies are digested only reluctantly . . . or are perhaps being sentenced to prohibition.

Whether they like it or not (and they are most likely to like it or even adore it), novel devotees are addicted to the novel's imagination/exaggerations/lies, provided the process and demands of such extravagance are technically controlled, without having any sort of moral discontent or without manifestly contradicting society's postulates.

Once the clash with society's postulates takes place, the novel "sells" exponentially, in an overt illustration of the dictum "the more lies poetry tells, the more beauty it brings about." With light modification of words and content, the quote reads, "The more unbounded novels are, the more beauty they bring about."

With a careful look at literature and art, and life as a whole, it seems that the sweetest of everything turns out to be the most untruthful and rebellious, commonly reinforced by this more famous saying: "The forbidden fruit always tastes the sweetest." Although life is full of pleasure within the realm of what is permitted in accordance with customs and ethics, literature and art still insist on raising the ornery question of why they are subject to a trial they didn't sign onto.

# One Lie Begets More Lies

In *Sudan Is My Land*, a collection of essays, Tayeb Salih described Francis Deng[14] as "a cosmopolitan with great knowledge of Arabic and high mastery of English. He is a writer and novelist who has the privilege novelists normally have to see things from different angles."

What concerns us the most in Salih's testimony about Francis Deng is its last segment, and more accurately, the very second sentence of the citation abstractly and not only for being expressed in favor of Mr. Deng. It is not surprising that Tayeb Salih has granted novelists the advantage of seeing things differently, given that he's a novelist eager to include his proposition as if talking about an axiom.

Is it true that novelists have the "aptitude/talent" of looking at things from more than one angle (regardless of Tayeb Salih's presumed bias)? In fact, novelists have it and more; they do master the art of "telling lies," as we have detailed in two previous essays. Without having any deliberate moral judgment, we would rather opt for "lies" if we want a more explicit term to replace "fantasy" (their pretext for committing falsity).

Laying Tayeb Salih's statement on the line for the sake of boldness/daring (which the great novelist definitely did not have in mind; what he thought about at that time was almost the opposite, i.e., that novelists had the ability to create great works should be received positively from a moral perspective), novelists have the competence to lie from more

---

[14] Francis Deng is a politician and diplomat from South Sudan who served as the newly independent country›s first ambassador to the United Nations from 2012 to July 2016. He has authored and edited forty books in the fields of law, conflict resolution, internal displacement, human rights, anthropology, folklore, history, and politics and has also written two novels on the theme of the crisis of national identity in the Sudan.

than one angle. The middle ground where the different opponents can meet may be summarized in the word "fantasy" being equivalent to (as we saw earlier) the morally palatable and aesthetically/artistically glorified "process of telling lies."

It is not that easy to go beyond the fact that once a reader finishes a novel, he is supposed to experience (in parallel with ecstasy) the feeling of abandonment because everything he has read is not real, even though it might be a higher expression of "the coveted truth," so to speak.

It seems that the novel's devotees are handling the "shock" of their disappointment—following a feverish passion for a wonderful novel they have just finished reading before they got back to reality anew—through sinking in further "novelistic lies" by engaging in other novels that would let them dive into the skies of desired truths. "Truth," in this respect, corresponds precisely to our interpretation about the meaning of looking at things from more than one angle, a feeling (and act) that accompanies novelists even outside the scope of their literary work (see the testimony of Tayeb Salih in regard to Francis Deng). Salih wanted to apply the same notion, as if it were an axiom, to all novelists.

This is then the recipe of "fighting fire with fire" that the supporters of the new trend (readers, critics, and novelists) cling to so as to protect them from the shocking effects of encountering reality as long as future novels, whatever "realism" they may claim, can fly far beyond fantasy.

The novel may acquire a status worthy of appreciation provided its devotees admit that when a novel tells lies, it does not do more than simulate reality. Instead, they insist on extravagant promises for a virtuous city where novelists prevail armed with the promise of a better reality. Therefore, the most accurate role that would make the novel, along with its leaders and apostates, worthy of potential esteem could have been advocated by those devotees as a "reorientation" of the message of life—which is already hard to decipher—not only for the purpose of indirect explanation and confirmation, but also, and mainly, through flying across the shores of imagination.

Only through this interpretation can the novel gain a privilege that poetry (specifically Arabic lyrical poetry) missed. Poetry was mainly obsessed with either direct preaching of wisdom or excessive reliance on description across the various forms/purposes of ancient Arabic poetry.

The privilege in question can be more explicit when perceived as an "inverted movement" aimed at making ethics more flexible so as to help people live in accordance with practical and acceptable "utilitarianism" with the least possible remorse. That interpretation is certainly more useful to the novel's devotees than the utopian claim that its raison d'être lies in paving the way for idealism (principles and dreams alike) to access the minds of people despite the bitter reality.

# The Novel for the Novel's Sake

It is (somehow) permissible for some of the novel's devotees to praise the narrative genre by analogy to "art for art's sake" as a principle; that is, there is no motive behind the surrender to the euphoria of the novel but embracing the new trend without having any deliberate or even spontaneous attention to grant it supremacy over other forms of literary writing, or over writing altogether. Proponents of the novel may perhaps have the right to prefer—spontaneously or deliberately— their narrative devotion over other forms of creative writing, but they are not permitted to reinforce the (privileged) literary brand as being worthy of exclusive reign over the current era in retaliation for poetry's domination (in terms of both space and time) throughout the Arabic literary tradition for more than ten centuries.

Nevertheless, it is common among novel lovers that they declare their affection through exclusion—the exclusion of the other competitors with a blow, and they'd rather it be a knockout. The novel's fiercest competitor still unwilling to come down (though staggering) is verse, referred to above and throughout this book. This is due to the fact that literary arts such as the story and the short story are not considered to be among the most blatant rebels. They easily fall within the novelistic camp when one is categorizing literary genres as either friend or foe.

Worst of all, respondents to the "epidemic fever" of following the trend (of loving novels) are basically found among critics and novelists and not among the members of the novel's devoted readers. Such readers resist pursuing the pleasure of a familiar art form, let alone spend much effort tasting other passions. They seem to be trying to escape an uncalculated adventure that might put their already palpable pleasure at risk.

Based on the foregoing, critics seem to be biased toward a particular literary genre even at the expense of banning the other existing genres, in case praise of the privileged category is not enough to keep people from the remaining creative writing genres; the literary category in question will end up topping the hierarchy. This is exactly what today's prominent critics are doing in favor of the novel.

Moreover, quite a few poets have abandoned poetry to curry favor with the novel (or at least have decided to experiment with writing narrative fiction more than once) in search of literary glory they couldn't find through verse (the most important phase of Arabic cultural heritage). Even today's critics are deserting poetry criticism to adopt the criticism of the most prevailing literary genre and, accordingly, the one with the highest potential to guarantee prominence.

The discovery of novelistic talents has become one of the critics' favorite missions, carrying it out as if they were saints preaching good conduct and warning against the disastrous consequences of evil. As far as literature is concerned, evil consists in everything existing independently outside the novelistic genre rather than being, according to the natural and logical definition, every work of poor value from an exclusively artistic point of view. This is true even when dealing with a well-known novel.

What makes the novel impose its authority to such an extent that it can effortlessly transcend the boundaries set by those in charge of assessing the different genres of literature? From this side, the novel seems to be a story of a real mass phenomenon which is too late to avoid (except for those who still cling to "literary orthodoxies"). It seems that all that can be done is to interpret the reasons behind the new sweeping wave, rather than to question its legitimacy to dominate. Besides, it seems that most of the critics pretend they are still committed to verse criticism as if they were reluctantly performing an indispensable ritual. These pretenders dissect (analyze) pieces of verse at their disposal with a hidden arrogance toward a literary genre that belongs (in their concealed opinion) to the past. They inevitably confirm the validity of the poems that prove to be soundly original, with much pity for the "poor poets," referring to them as being "right men at the wrong time." I avoid mentioning that the statement in question actually reads "wrong men in the right time" on account that the novel is the "manifest destiny" of the present time whose authority must take over everybody, though not necessarily through the perspective of "the novel for the novel's sake."

# Thank God 1 Got Out!

I proclaimed, somewhere in this book, an armistice with the novel being one of the literary arts I am not much fond of. I have often resorted to peace when there is a good reason for a ceasefire, like when inadvertently finding a creatively elaborate novel or when noticing the success of a young novelist shedding light on a social/cultural wasteland.

The accidental truce, as mentioned above, helps me take a breath for a while to read a good novel under the shade of peace, pausing my vicious campaign against narrative fiction basically in the sense that it is regarded as a prevailing "fashion." As it might be deduced, my struggle against the novel is a one-sided war, and perhaps, to be precise, a conflict between one party (me) and a group of parties (the novel along with its writers, critics, readers, and publishers), with no idea about the existence of the war I have waged. I am afraid, in this context, I have become like the well-known knight who fought windmills in the belief that they were the source of all evil in this world. Although I am deploying this analogy only ironically, such a view is plausible provided my crisis with the novel is perceived as a battle against the novelistic genre per se and not as an opposition to the dominance of a particular literary category over almost every possible space of literary creativity. It's the same way a haircut or robe prevails over the world of fashion as a privileged trend worthy of the interest of eager teenagers (girls and boys alike).

During the moments of peace under the shade of the new trend, I sometimes come to fall in love with a novel; but, thank God, I quickly recover from the grip of that admiration as soon as I sense it is paving the path of seduction under my feet so that it can drive me to where the other "opponents" have been enslaved by the same ecstasy of that art to the extent that they can behold the beauty of any of the existing literary creative forms.

The amazing words of the novel are similar to the "abracadabra" (as in the English version of the term "magic"). The fall into the trap of a wonderful novel is similar to slipping into the snare of a cunning magician whose tricks smartly deceive, leaving the viewer/beholder with nothing to resort to but applause and admiration. In fact, this is an attribute of magnificent literature (art in general), and poetry is perhaps more eligible than the novel to receive such an honor. However, the time of the reign of verse over literary charm has declined after a long period. Once upon a time (I'm speaking of Arabic literature specifically), the "abracadabra" used to be verses of poetry uttered by a poet (a magical architect of words) already confident that his listeners would be taken by his uniquely captivating magic/charm.

The magic of the novel is, accordingly, not due to special artistic merits or purely divine gifts engendering its exclusive ability to seduce, but because of the (literary) privilege it has been granted so it can spread its wings across the wide open air at the expense of the other (marginalized) arts. This deliberate process of coronation was held by those who saw in the crowned genre a literary trend worthy not only of supremacy, but also, and specifically, of the eligibility to be the only contestant in the race. Supporters of such a monarchy are readers and novelists who keep glorifying the novel (the Dictator)—along with the consequences it brings about—crying "Long live the king!"

The magic of the novel—as a close friend has sympathetically responded to my malaise in reaction to the proclaimed "Novel's Era"— is the surrender of the public to the charm of "Once upon a time," with its fascinating power to attract the ears of listeners (even those with scarce sensitivity) and drive them up till the end of the tale (which mustn't lack ingenuity) in order to ultimately satisfy their curiosity. This achievement is out of reach simply because new inquisitiveness will arise anew from between the seeds of a new narrative whose predecessors proved that people's ears (and hearts) are so keen on that art of (story)telling being the most capable among literary forms to tickle the instinctive sense already existing in every descendent of Adam and Eve. The almost unique authority in question is manifested not only in satisfying curiosity but also in stimulating appetite with every new tale, even when it is merely the offspring of pure fantasy.

34

# The Novel and Sex

There is no great novel that is free from sex and excitement, while poorly written novels are almost centered around eroticism and excitement. Is this a mere coincidence?

It is hard to believe that the matter is no more than a coincidence. Sex has always been regarded as a strong means for arousing stimulation and satisfying curiosity (and regenerating it anew at the same time). It is even more surprising that tales and legends about sex permeate novels published in societies not suffering from sexual deprivation. Nevertheless, such novels do quite well compared to the effect similar narrative fiction has on societies (within the most conservative countries) that abide sexual repression.

In fact, there is a difference worthy of consideration (being honest and fair in analysis) when tackling the role of sex in the promotion of a novel. In liberal societies in different parts of the world, especially the West, sex renders a good novel more attractive. In sexually repressed societies, sex is, on the other hand, almost a major source of attraction for novels including the ones lacking originality. Since most, if not all, of the repressed societies are less advanced in literature and generally in every possible aspect of life, it is possible to find out why sex alone can contribute to the (massive) spread of weak or even aesthetically mediocre novels. However, the role sex plays (in Western societies) in terms of giving an artistically well-woven novel added value deserves being investigated with deep reflection.

In the West, before getting into the most controversial phases of the subject matter, it must first be recognized that sex, when skillfully injected into a good novel, can be a valid reason justifying the greater demand for the piece of work in question. The demand for such a novel may be attributed to curiosity about sex per se or, otherwise, to the incorporation of the captivating phenomenon that is a "basic instinct" in the life of human beings.

In Western social contexts, once again—where social freedom and perspectives of creativity are so broad for any sort of novels to flourish— the matter adds dimensions of excitement when dealing with forbidden sexual relations according to the traditions of those societies, basically incest and adultery. (This is adultery not only within the institution of marriage, but also among any two parties in a relationship that allows for sexual intercourse according to the social conventions of those communities.) Nevertheless, given the generally well-known rigor in assessing any (literary) piece of work in the West, the inclusion of sex— even with the most extreme and peculiar stimuli—is still associated with artistic skill, if the author aspires to success and renown.

The only case in which the West waives its customary sternness (when it comes to work in general and in regard to the standards of judging literary/artistic works specifically) rises when the literary/ artistic piece is in conflict with the traditions of a conservative society, and created by a writer who belongs to that society. Thus, artistically modest eroticism can help promote a literary piece of work—aesthetically feeble in itself—that discusses the issues of religion or women on the basis of an overt approach of rivalry and hostility.

Accordingly, sex is much more effective compared to the other (human) instincts that do not, necessarily, guarantee success for a poorly written novel; nor does it bring more glitter for a novel already doing well on the path of seduction. In this context, I am not intending to juxtapose sex and food/drink in accordance with the famous Islamic rule about fasting as an act of "abstaining from foods, drinks, and intimate intercourse from dawn to sunset." I would rather compare sex to the instincts of fear, revenge, curiosity, possessiveness, and many more that are supposed to contend with the appetites for sex and food exclusively stated in the above mentioned definition about fasting.

There are novels, whether great or modest, that revolve around sexual excitement. Sex, however, has always been present to intersperse another central (independent) theme in narrative fiction. This may be another instinct, such as revenge or belligerence, or a complex set of instincts. Nevertheless, it is not precisely the instinct tackled in the narrative that draws attention, but rather the idea and the process of events. The most decisive and appealing point of the instinct in the novel—both in its center and on its brilliant surroundings—is achieved only when sex is involved.

Thus, sex within the novelistic experience seems to deserve being singled out not only as a "basic instinct," but basically as the absolute "essential instinct" in narrative fiction. Here we can make an analogy between novel and poetry (being comparatively chaste). Verse transcends instincts in its permanent search for new/distant horizons of spirituality. Sex scarcely showed up from between the verses of the "apostate poets," whereas it has broken into novels across their wide-open gates, crowning the heads of novelists with fame and glory.

# In the Presence of Sir Marquez Himself

The role of exceptional artists—of any category of art—is vital to the spread and immortality of that art, having been ushered in, of course, by glorious pioneers, though not necessarily being the best among their successors who will emerge, later on, as practitioners of the same (creative) expertise. Thus is the familiar (though not necessarily determined) relationship between pioneering and excellence, which by virtue of the nature of things grants preference to some artists among the new generation so they attain prominence by taking advantage of the building blocks (and not necessarily the foundation) that the predecessors already established in the groundwork of artistic creativity. This shouldn't constitute an absolute standard governing the assessment of proficiency of a successor compared to a predecessor or vice versa, given that the matter about artistic leadership is, generally, less likely to engender much controversy.

The role of great artists in consolidating and promoting their art is so significant for two reasons. The first is the effect of stardom on people in principle; the masses would learn by heart many an extract from the autobiography of a writer despite the fact that most of them did not read any of the pieces of work by the writer in question. The second reason lies in the magic of proficiency/mastery on those (as in my case) who would engage in perceiving exquisite craftsmanship, even if they might be obviously antagonistic to that category of art.

In light of the above, it would not be strange for one, like me, to be captivated by the charm of novelistic creativity reading any of the works by Gabriel Garcia Marquez, bearing in mind my repeatedly proclaimed indignation at the "fashion of the time" on more than one ground. My stand is mainly centered on my view that great works (literary, artistic, or otherwise creative—even in the purely practical aspects of human genius) can never be subject to a seemingly superficial notion such as "fashion," though my interaction with the said "new trend" reveals the fact that it has got a more concrete role and effect in life than we might think being armed with our overconfident scrutiny.

The other noteworthy reason for my caution vis-à-vis the novel is probably derived from my original background as a poet—and later as an essayist/writer who would rather fly away out of the cage of storytelling. If ever fiction is strongly inevitable, it can be approached through essay writing. It is worthy of being the most "fashionable," among all genres, throughout every possible literary period.

Despite all that has been said so far, the glamour of the novel remains valid for me through exceptional novelists such as Tayeb Salih and Garcia Marquez. I have repeatedly praised Salih for being considered worthy of the remarkable reputation and glory he achieved. And Marquez already reached the highest possible prestige and acclaim that no novelist has been granted so far—a huge and worthy gain indeed.

Along with mastery/proficiency broadly agreed on, many reasons congregated for the completion of the Colombian writer's unique myth. At the forefront of these reasons is that the novelist belongs to a South American country not among the most advanced or famous on the continent, despite his long stay in Mexico (investigating the geographical boundaries of the continent), the most affluent and famous city northward. Marquez had the chance to befriend prominent revolutionary leaders like Fidel Castro and, later on, less rebellious political personalities or modernity advocates such as Bill Clinton. Before I conclude with charisma and presentability in terms of character and name as a strange reason to consolidate the myth, I would like to refer to the intrinsic and less controversial reasons manifested in Spanish, a language notorious for such a uniquely viable creativity owing to its particularity compared to English, French, Italian, and German (prestigiously known for their competence and predominance in this respect). Spanish has incomparably spread in the West and the East alike—Arabic being among the "defeated" languages. The mother tongue in which the work is written has a great magical/authoritative effect not only after the piece of work is translated to many other languages, but also before the translation takes place. First, it helps the writer draw inspiration (consciously and unconsciously) from a whole linguistic tradition in letter and spirit while writing. Second, language (Spanish in this context), especially if it is prominently popular, can attract double the readers, critics, and obsessive devotees on the grounds that the race to the (literary) podium is exclusively between exceptionally good works.

Marquez himself would grant me the opportunity to escape the temptation of the novel before I shall claim my evasion from the said sedition/seduction thanks to my almost (if I may say) innate predilection for other forms of creativity other than (short or long) narrative fiction. The compass of my devotion would rather diverge to the essay form along with the wide horizons of critical articles/reviews. Besides, my annoyance (disgust?) at the fervent spread of the novel might seem like an artificial reason that fuses tenacious pretense with true spontaneity. This apparent contradiction does not question the sincerity of my ardent will of emancipation from captivity of the novel, nor would it reinforce its entitlement to take over all forms of creative writing.

Marquez is giving me that chance because he is a professionally gifted essayist in principle; journalism was not merely a transient in his writing career, but rather a pivotal obsession before and during his unique fame. On the other hand (and for the same reason), my stand in regard to narrative fiction (in particular, the novel) may look unjustified on the basis that a great novelist can also be a distinguished essayist, though Marquez's essays are not as great as his fiction when both are viewed as the epitome of exceptional creativity. Therefore, it would be safer for me to cling to the assertion that my (mortal) enmity toward the "new trend" (the novel) is primarily a cry against the entrenched "fever" among writers and readers alike.

# The Invention of Lying

*The Invention of Lying* is a 2009 American fantasy romantic comedy film written and directed by Ricky Gervais. The film stars Gervais as the first human with the ability to lie in a world where people can only tell the truth. The hero lied when the cashier in the bank asked him about his account balance because the computers went down. An idea (reaction) came to his mind that he should say he had $800 instead of the real sum of $300. He was in urgent need of the $800 to avoid being kicked out of his house. Thus, according to the film, the first lie in human history was begotten. Lying was so unlikely at that time that, even when the malfunction was repaired, the cashier had no doubt about the man's honesty despite the computer's confirming the false claim.

It wasn't strange, then, that the sparkling temptation of lying kept seducing the hero's mind. He came to discover that this new invention could be more useful than the pursuit of his personal interests. He might be able to save his friend from being arrested for drunk driving, to convince his neighbor not to commit suicide, and to help his mother await death (which her doctor coldly described as very imminent) happily, considering that what she was waiting for was a better life and not the infinite nothingness she was horribly scared of.

Our greatest concern in relation to the manifestations of the new invention would be how the hero (a scriptwriter in the story) was inspired with captivating ideas to revive his collapsing professional and, consequently, financial aspirations to the extent of leading him to invent lies. The special mission that was responsible for the failure of the hero's career started when he was assigned to write a screenplay about the fourteenth-century boring life. He took advantage of the magical invention to embrace new perspectives of success that had been completely repressed before. Thus he could successfully rewrite the (hi)story of the fourteenth-century boring life anew—inventing a tale of astronauts who invaded the earth at that time and wiped out the memory of all human beings.

One of the most impressive gestures in the film is that it defers the idea of the invention (discovery) of lying to the modern age, maybe due to aesthetic requirements, including the double chances of finding paradoxes and the pleasure of overcoming the challenges of transcendence in the basis and details of the work. The fictional narrative does not oppose the probability that lying could have existed before the fourteenth century and then faded along with what was lost of human memory during the supposed space attack.

Practically, we know that the history of lying is far older than this. It is, after all, impossible to discover the exact start of lying in history, which is why the subject is handled through comedy. And if the story is a comedy blended with some seriousness (and innocence?) to track the history of the first lie, our objective in what follows is to consider novelistic lying in connection with the truthfulness that surrounds other literary arts, such as the essay, without wiping away the novel's appeal and beauty. Still, we cannot deny the importance of lying in literature and art (and life?) in general.

Humans don't have to lie to achieve attractiveness. However, the fact that cannot be ignored is that lying gives people more charm, and so is the case with the novel . . . and art in general.

Accordingly, some people should not be driven to rush to confirm that the fifteenth century witnessed the birth of the modern novel with Miguel de Cervantes and his *Don Quixote*, or even before, with the Greeks and others. In fact, the early emergence of the novel started with the new human invention of lying. The above-mentioned movie surprisingly does not only ratify the conclusion (about the correlation between inventing lying and the appearance of the novel) to the extent of complete matching, but it also goes further. It supports the idea that humans reached the conclusion that the novel is one of the noticeable fruits of the invention of lying. On the other side, the emergence of the essay as a creative art seems, through tracking its roots, somehow similar in the sense that it started with the invention of speech. So when essays incorporate some instances of lying, it is because of what sneaked into them after the invention of the novel as a new literary genre in specific and not after the invention of lying. The novel thereby is the first party to teach essays how to tell lies—a rare example of how a mother was spoiled by her daughter through the latter's twisted demeanor.

The essay, as a category of creative writing, does not seem to be the offspring of the novel even in terms of quantity. It is hard for people like me to concede even supposedly that the novel can encompass all of the word arts, as its supporters claim. In this context, being guided by straight logic, we can say that the novel was growing till it exceeded the size of its mother—the essay. Here, we do not need to reverse the logic to justify the seemingly prospering offspring at the expense of its deep roots where it first saw the light.

A deliberate consideration of literary genres leads to the fact that the novel is the "prodigal" offspring of the essay in the sense that the latter is the true root of the unrhymed literary pieces before they became spoilt by lying and fantasy (the short story and the novel). This is like when a balloon swells and it looks beautiful and grand, though it contains nothing but air.

In fact, that is the flashiness of narrative art: readers need only prick to discover the (balloon) illusion they inherit from that type of writing when it comes to precious ideas and insight. But the essay is free from the bounds of such an illusion provided essayists do not shift into courtliness toward the reader through the fad of lying. This may take place with the insertion of some of the garments of fantasy and adulation in favor of narrative genres that are widespread in the writing market these days.

Indeed, the novel may have the right to be taken in the dizziness of vanity that usually accompanies literary pleasure acquired through the tickling sweet words and the nonsense of the funny imagination, stretching without constrains of rhyme or rhythm and invading (literary) markets. Therefore, the novel is the master in the literary scene, but not in a way that transcends the mastership of poetry when it comes to rhyme or rhythm as the criteria of the competition. Indeed, poetry excels in bringing about the most sublime expressions, along with the purest and sweetest conceptions. Besides, the seeming leadership of the novel cannot take over the authority of the essay, which affords precious thoughts fueling the readers' imagination through the use of expressions selected with much creativity and freedom in the fields of literature and creative writing as a whole.

The "official" statistics stated in encyclopedias and reference books advocate antecedence of the essay form compared to the novelistic genre. However, the other factor, more important than antecedence in terms of time, is the antecedence in fluency of expression and the ability to contain meanings away from the supremacy of "the new trend" that now dominates.

# Novelists Believed Their Own Woven Lie(s)!

The most serious moral crime Arab poets are said to have committed is that they "say things they don't actually do," even though this form of falsehood was not intended for pledge breaching, but for the overestimation of the self and the ally, or even for undermining the value of the opponent. It was only after the coming of Islam that those earlier practices were claimed as ethical offenses. And indeed, those unexercised words were (and we will soon see that they are still) the secret behind the charm and glamour of poetry. However, the agreement of Arabs on the deceptive seduction of poetry, especially after this was endorsed in light of the new morals that Islam had ushered in, did not completely save people from the sedition of verse, but they were saved from it to the extent that they shifted away to practicing and learning the new religion. Meanwhile, the ember of poetry was still lit up deep in their souls, awaiting the chance to have it soaring again under any practical pretext. When that happened with the rise of a new form of the Islamic state during the Umayyad Era, the start was not accompanied with the forfeiting of the moral values that the flourishing Islam had laid down. It was initiated by ignoring rigid obedience while submitting to the condemnation of falsehood, on condition that this submission be overt, bypassing objections to considering poetry as an "inevitable evil." Thus, holders of the ember of principles had no other option but to admit that "poetry is a beautiful evil."

Even strict literal supporters of religious principles admit that "poetic evil" (the term they prefer) incorporates numerous instances of beauty. Nowadays many preachers cite verses from the finest poetry (always in connection with the claim that the more lies it tells, the more beauty it brings about); then afterward they come to proclaim their reservations—either because the quoted poetry contains "sins" (as interpreted by the strict religious view) or because of the poet himself (viewed as having an unsavory reputation with regard to the literal interpretation of the Islamic doctrines in terms of speech in general—not specifically poetry).

Arab poets used to tell lies and people liked their lies while being conscious that they were lies. I do not quite believe that any of the ancient Arab poets fell victim believed their own lies in any of their poems. The ones who were the most likely to believe such lies were the praised, either individuals or tribes. The matter here seems as if it is reversed in some way, in that the poet did not invent the lie, but he explicitly expressed the feelings of his praised party, individuals and communities, through only deploying his creative potency to respond to that desire beautifully and clearly. . . . The praised party was to blame for any untruthfulness, not the poet; he was merely the genius medium whereby that dulcet lying could be woven so dexterously.

That was the case with the Arabic lyrical poetry, whereas poetry of the preceding and following nations who were familiar with theatrical poetry is another poetic variation that should be considered from a perspective of creative writing, mainly relying on imagination. This can rightly lead us to raise the question whose response is the title of this essay: "Have novelists believed their lie?" This question seems to be a result of belief in a consensus that lying in novels is so flagrant that it does not need any justification. Poetic lies constitute a sort of inevitable instance of creative exaggeration meant to emphasize and beautify the intended meaning.

Novelists probably lie to the extent that they can hardly escape the dominance of their fabricated world, only to embrace another lie through which they can invent another different world. In this, they are similar to actors who play a character in one story before moving to distinct roles in other stories. The big difference in this context is that the novelist incarnates the whole story and not only one character. Having this in mind, novelists can be regarded as the masters of lying not only among creative writers, but among all the practitioners of all types of arts. In fact, their job description is basically built not only on lying but on their ingenuity in depicting a lie as if it were really a truth.

In the Arabic version of *Why We Write*, the American writer of detective novels David Baldacci recounts his childhood: "I was imagining worlds all the time, small worlds where I lose myself inside. I recounted my stories to many of those who wanted to hear them and to those who did not want to." He went on: "I wrote the best of my novels when I was a lawyer. Do you know who wins in the court? It is the client who is represented by a lawyer who tells better stories than the other lawyer. When you are litigating, you cannot change the facts, you can just reorder them to make the story support the case of your client, valuing certain matters and undermining others, making sure that the facts you want people to believe are the most convincing, and you dispose of those facts that can potentially be harmful to your case either through justifying or hiding them. This is how stories are told."[15]

As a child, Baldacci lied explicitly and spontaneously wove stories out of lies. He later came back as a lawyer to say that winning litigation is not related to inventing facts but rather to reordering them. But this doesn't take into account that reordering facts is likely an invented definition (devious/elusive) of lying. Besides, hiding parts of some facts is the same as outright lying.

The most important issue we are concerned with in relation to lying at this point is not what is taking place in David Baldacci's courtrooms but in his detective novels, especially after he left lawyering to dedicate his entire focus to lying without any constraint—to inventing facts instead of "nobly" hiding behind reordering them or keeping some of them in secret.

Pragmatism comes at the top of the job descriptions for lawyers. The purpose is, in short, saving the client, even if guilty. It is pragmatism graced by the force of law. Far away from Baldacci and his profession, which he left after it had inspired him to write many of his creative pieces, we notice that novelists usually do not need to make their start from any profession that may help them invent their stories begotten from the womb of a lie. Instead, it arises from a "crude" soul who sees, in the power to create falsehood (literary lies), a mission worthy of submission

---

[15] Meredith Maran, ed., *Why We Write: 20 Acclaimed Authors on How and Why They do What They Do* (New York: Penguin Group, 2013).

and ovation, especially when it potentially results in discovering a talent that may blossom legendary achievement(s) deserving public praise.

However, the lies of novelists did not turn on them as magic may sometimes turn on the magicians. Such a flip-flop was eagerly anticipated by a provoked person (like me?) to take over the legendary success of the novel nowadays. But what happened in reality was the opposite. People's immersion in devouring "tasty" lies gave the novelists more enthusiasm and more determination to persist on their path, tempted by the idea that people's perception of literary arts won't proceed healthily unless the novel is in the lead.

# The Reader as Accomplice

The novel's nefarious domination over the literary scene in specific and over creative writing in general couldn't have been within reach without the collusion on the part of readers who insatiably, and without having any scruples, gobble narrative fiction, ignoring all other categories of writing and speech arts alike.

According to business owners (publishers in this case), a successful piece of product, regardless of any other proclamation that the losers may drawl, is one that attracts more consumers. The word "losers" in this context denotes the loss of "market(s)" despite claiming the possession of good merchandise, whose only defect lies in lacking public interest on the part of the audience(s).

Because we are concerned here with readers rather than with publishers, we proceed with the first counterpart to notice that they (readers) perpetrate their love for novels with premeditation and relish. In fact, what they consider blemish in the essay (in some of its cases) at the level of the strange use of language, is warmly welcomed when it comes to the fantasy of novels. As for the weird choice of themes, it represents the narrative trick whereby readers are hunted as prey. I will not have any serious objection here provided weird topics are meant to address social or moral taboos or any other similar thematic considerations. Apparently, the debate has never been about measuring the spread among writing arts (even though some may think the opposite) but about how the approach to the subject matter(s) is carried out.

Apart from what is considered morally, socially, religiously, or politically shocking, writers and publishers alike are surprised by the readers' gourmand devotion to strange topics such as wave motion (physics), which not only propagandized *The Perfect Storm* as a realistic novel but also incited the making of a movie, with the same title, starring George Clooney.

In the Arabic version of *Why We Write*, Sebastian Junger, the author of *The Perfect Storm*, stated: "I do this sort of explicit distinction when I'm writing. I'm very aware that I'm writing for (presumed) readers, and I do everything I can to engage them, to make my writing accessible and compelling. At the same time, I try to be completely disinterested in what I think people will like. I'm writing for myself. I want to learn about the world, and writing is the way I do it. You can never determine people's tastes anyway. No one could have predicted *Perfect Storm* would be a hit, a fishing boat sinking in a storm? Neither the publishers know nor do readers; nobody knows how it happened."

With a little more update talking about the oddity of the idea, Junger proceeds: "In every book that I wrote there were moments I thought that: I can't insert this topic. I will lose half of my readers. In *The Perfect Storm*, the topic was about wave motion; how would anyone like to read about this? But I said to myself: the story needs that simply because the waves drowned the boat. You have to explain how waves work. Thus I made use of physics. If no one reads it, let it be. It will not be the end of my life anyway. If I cannot succeed as a writer, it will be always possible for me to go back to trees."[16] Sebastian Junger then continued: "I will write the best book that I can write. However, in case I am dealing with a topic I know readers cannot stand perceiving, I work on my language with extra effort to make them eat spinach. I don't like spinach but if you put enough garlic I will eat it."

Do all novelists and popular writers tackle the strangest themes in their work by adding more garlic? Perhaps yes, but garlic seems not to be enough of a magical spice to endure the (bitter) oddity of nonfiction writings for Arabs in specific. This leads to the conclusion that ignoring the other types of writing in favor of the novel was deliberate for the sake of propagandizing the new trend, a new "innovative accessory" for summer or winter of this year as a result of people's weariness about poetry's tyranny over Arab literary tastes for centuries. But what happened is that after decades of stumbling attempts by the other narrative genres, the markets of literature have submissively been taken

---

[16] Junger worked as a high climber for tree removal companies.

over by the novel (even at the expense of the story and the short story), not only as a seasonal fashion for summer or winter but basically as an ongoing trend, as most of the critics love to underline. Publishers couldn't believe that, at last, "something" written has brought back glamour to the book market, so they could not resist blessing it regardless of its genre.

Where do readers exactly stand concerning the above phenomenon? In fact, the reader is the one who ultimately ratifies the promotion by the critics and the media and executed by the publishers, though cautiously in the start. It is worth mentioning that the ratification process occurs sometimes while the readers themselves are surprised by what they are assenting to. This is the opposite of what happens in other situations where the readers are ready to assent to a category of creativeness they are already acquainted with, either from the same familiar genre or another genre that is still a new product to the literary markets in terms of the number of centuries it has existed.

In the book we quoted from earlier, Sebastian Junger states: "When you are at the ranking that you could be on the Times Bestseller lists, that's part of your work. There are very formidable books which did not enter the list, while fully ridiculous ones are included. Every writer and every person knows that entering (and remaining for the longest time possible in) the list does not rely entirely on the work quality." Here we add to Sebastian's words that entering the bestseller lists does not depend completely on the quality of what is written, but hugely on the nature of what is written regarding the genre to which it belongs. Readers are being prepared to welcome the best-selling, thus they become accomplices in the crime of disregarding what is written in the other luckless genres. Precisely, the matter is so because readers tend to submit to the march towards the direction dictated by the compasses in the hands of the critics, the media and the publishers.

# The Illusion of Imagination in Novels

"'One morning, when Gregor Samsa woke from troubled dreams, he found himself transformed in his bed into a horrible vermin. . . .' When I read the line I thought to myself that I didn't know anyone was allowed to write things like that," Garcia Marquez said. "If I had known, I would have started writing a long time ago."

That is what Gabriel García Marquez said to *Paris Review* magazine in an interview with Peter H. Stone. The words of the most prominent writer in Latin America were then translated into Arabic by Mohamed Aldhaba in a book entitled *Date a Girl Who Loves Writing.*

It was Franz Kafka who surprised Garcia Marquez that he was about to fall from his bed when he read the introductory sentence in "The Metamorphosis."

Garcia Marquez talked about his experience at the University of Bogota where he got in touch with a group of friends who introduced him to contemporary writers: "So I immediately started writing short stories which were basically the fruit of my readings. By then, I had not found the magical connection between literature and life yet. The stories were published in the literary section of *El Espectador* (newspaper) in Bogota and they did have a certain success at the time—probably because nobody in Colombia was writing like I was doing. My stories were mostly dedicated to depicting social issues along with countryside life. I was even told that my early pieces of work were largely influenced by the works of James Joyce."

Garcia Marquez's statement above is so surprising because it uncovers the fact that the prestigious magic realism writer was not born with a stock of imagination, as readers taken by the sublime story of Remedios's ascension to heaven in *One Hundred Years of Solitude* might have thought. "When I was writing about the journey of beautiful Remedios," says Garcia Marquez, "it took me long time to make it believable. One day, I went to the garden and saw a woman who used to come to our house to do the laundry. She was putting the bed sheets outside to dry while winds were blowing. The woman was talking to the strong winds as if begging them not to take the sheets away. I thought thus I would help beautiful Remedios ascend if I make use of the sheets. This is how I did it and everyone believed me. The main concern of every writer is how to convince the readers. A novelist can do anything he wants so long as he makes people believe in it."

In the above interview, Gustavo Arellano considers the best of what Garcia Marquez has written, revealing the magic recipe that can make everything believable in literature (perhaps talking about the novel in specific). Arellano said, "There is a sort of journalistic style in the manner you narrate. When you describe a supernatural event, for example, you tend to expatiate on details showing the timeline minute by minute in a way that gives the event much credibility. Can we say this is due to your being a journalist?"

Garcia Marquez said, "Yes, that's a journalistic trick which you can also apply to literature. For example, if you say that there are elephants flying in the sky, people are not going to believe you. But if you say that there are four hundred and twenty-five elephants flying in the sky, people will probably believe you. *One Hundred Years of Solitude* is full of that sort of trick."

Gabriel Garcia Marquez seems to address magical realism literature more than any other literary genre deploying imagination (fantasy). In fact, it is because there is no specific category of literature or narrative writing that relies only and exclusively on fantasy. In this context, Garcia Marquez says that "it always amuses me that the biggest praise for my work comes for the imagination, while the truth is that there's not a single line in all my work that does not have a basis in reality." What Garcia Marquez said here applies not only to magical realism but also to all literary and artistic work founded on imagination (science fiction, detective fiction, horror, fantasy, and so on).

"The problem," said Garcia Marquez about his fantastical writing, "is that Caribbean reality resembles the wildest imagination." We come to the realization that fantasy, to a large extent, resides in the crude concepts, not in what novelists write in their stories—plots so tough to believe.

I wrote in "Wisdom Highway"[17] that "All that is imaginable can be reachable; and only what no instance of imagination can reach is unperceivable." Thereby, we can say that there is nothing inimitable except for things that cannot be fantasized. In fact, I am not quite obsessed with confirming what Marquez stated about the importance of finding the thread(s) that connect(s) imaginary stories with reality (life) so as to make them plausible. I am much more concerned with what lies behind his statement: "The Caribbean reality portrays the wildest imagination," while reality in general portrays the most slippery instances of imagination. Garcia Marquez has chosen the Caribbean reality simply because, after all, it was there where he was born and brought up. These are myths that specialists and writers exaggeratedly describe as being deeply allusive while those myths are no more than palpable instances of people's life everywhere under the roof of this world. They are undoubtedly truths whose fantasy is rooted in the fact that they do not occur every day and to whomever.

Novel custodians hereby exaggerate in amplifying fantasy as a notion existing outside reality. They proclaim that their sacred genre can invent charm that no other creative writing (including Arabic lyric poetry and the essay) can challenge whenever the contest is about the concept of the literary work as a whole rather than the rhetorical images that weave through the web of the narrative in question. Fantasy, as we have seen above, in the words of the most famous novelists, is, above all, a sound (and indispensable) connection to real life.

Referring, once again, to my "Wisdom Highway," we can conclude that we usually imagine things that might come true in another place and time, in the past, present, or future, either around where we live or even million light-years away. Therefore, narrative fiction (that is, the novel) has no divine secret to reign over the other creative speech and writing genres.

---

[17] A book published in Arabic by the author (04/08/2012).

# The Unholy Fantasy

It is unwise, and even illogical, to underestimate the (huge) impact of imagination in the novel and literature in general. The novel's prevail has been fundamentally due to the use of fantasy. Similarly, the other (literary) genres derive, in one way or another, their charm and grace from embracing the perspectives of imagination. Nevertheless, the reverence of imagination on the part of novel devotees (novelists and readers alike) must be undermined and refuted.

Gabriel Garcia Marquez reacted to the matter when he said "it always amuses me that the biggest praise for my work comes for the imagination, while the truth is that there's not a single line in all my work that does not have a basis in reality." The words of the Colombian novelist denote that imagination has a concrete (not an ethereal) connection to reality. In truth, real life is not only a source from which creators/artists extract the nectar of their creativity, but it is also the reservoir that keeps fueling them whenever they run out of inspiration and insight.

To be fair, we should confess that there exists a reciprocal exchange between imagination and reality. Reality provides imagination with the indispensable fuel for the takeoff. Some of the fruits of imagination grow to become parts of real life enriching the already existing truths. Thus, considerable phases of reality have resulted from the accumulation of what used to be merely pure fantasy throughout periods of the past.

Accordingly, narrative fiction, along with the other creative writing forms, is guilty when it considers that imagination is so holy that any piece of writing is not even part of literature if not established in imagination. Besides, it is unfair to question the aesthetic quality of a literary work according to the degree to which fantasy occupies the work. Imagination is not the only tool to guarantee originality and creativity; there are many literary ingredients that can help beget exceptional writing without having to be at the mercy of the demands of fantasy.

At this point, we are hard-pressed to come up with a clear definition of imagination. This mission will be even harder when we realize that there is not only one sort of imagination, but many. The uneasiness then will be laid in differentiating between the contrastive notions about imagination across the impassable path leading to a comprehensive and definite definition whose basic utility is to briefly refer to the phenomenon whenever it is necessary.

More importantly, we will discover the unique relationship between imagination and creativity, which most of people confusingly consider to be synonymous. To distinguish between the two dictums, we can say that it is possible to come across an original creativity not only without excessive imagination but without any imagination at all. Here I am not going to cite great critical and intellectual works as illustration of creativity but rather literary pieces of work based on creative ideas and completely realistic methods of expression.

If imagination stands for tackling what hasn't been approached yet, it can be then considered as the other side of the same coin of creativity. However, it is most of the time referred to as what can't be concretized (on the ground of real life), while it is widely agreed upon that creativity is that masterpiece (in whatever genre) flourishingly coming to life after having been nothing but an abstract notion.

Even though he had underestimated the value of mental effort to produce marvelous work without basically relying on imagination, the words of Sebastian Junger in *Why We Write* confirm that the creation of an appealing work does not necessarily mean following in the steps of imagination in total subservience: "My writing does not belong to narrative literature. So I don't need to brainstorm my mind to produce new ideas. My best ideas come from the world. I reap them but I don't need to create them. All that I have to do is taking things that I saw, things that people told me, and things I looked for myself, the making of the world. Then I transform them into a concatenation of words that people would like to read. Writing, this wonderful alchemy, magic-like will be read if you do it the right way."

Junger's job as a journalist, a war correspondent, helps him see that the needed "brainstorming" to produce unliterary writing is much easier than anything else. Even though the value of a literary work should not be assessed in relation to the required mental effort, but with the dexterity that manifests in its writing process, original intellectual creativity (even in the non-narrative work) usually needs tremendous mental activity. The core issue is not necessarily about the purpose behind imagination as commonly dealt with, but about the unique and original creation/invention of some like-no-other literary (or any creative) piece of work.

The most important part of Sebastian Junger's contribution in the above-mentioned book concerning the relationship between imagination and reality is best conveyed when he says: "In journalism there is a separating line between imagination and reality. I feel that I have to hold to it. As a journalist you can't imagine a scene or a conversation. While in the middle of writing *The Perfect Storm*, I faced a dreadful critical situation. I was writing about a boat that disappeared, but I lost the thread when the boat left the coast. What to say about a boat that sank, where did it happen? What would people be saying to each other? What would death be like on a boat drowned by a storm? It seemed as if I had a deep hole in the midst of the narration process. I couldn't fill the missing part resorting to imagination."

That hole in the narration, as Junger described it, was supposed to be a factor for other writers to unlimitedly embrace the seductive bells of imagination. But Sebastian simply and daringly faced his inability to imagine. It was not the end of the world for weaving a marvelous book: "I took all my writing experience from reading good works by other writers including Thomas, Wolf, Peter Matheson, John McPhee, and Richard Preston. The latter also faced the same problem in *The Hot Zone*. His main character died resulting in holes in the plot line which were filled with suppositions. He told the reader: "we don't know. Perhaps he (the main character) said this, perhaps he did that. We know that his temperature was $41°C$ ($105.8°F$). That's why he felt this.'"

Junger went on proving his bravery and simplicity in facing his impotency in relation to imagination: "I realized that I could suggest realistically possible scenarios to my readers without lying (a precise expression of imagination!) as long as I am honest about mere possibilities that we take into account, keeping it within the range of journalism. So, I found other boats that survived the storm and I listened to their calls through the radio. I could have said: 'We don't know what happened to the boat of my fellows, but we know what happened to another boat. I met a person whose boat capsized in heavy seas. He found his lungs full of air in a sinking boat. Based on this incident, he told me about what he thought had happened to the crew of the *Andrea Gail*. This is how I managed to narrate it to the readers. I filled the gaps utilizing logic, not fantasy. Thus responding to this (critical) issue was very exciting for me."

As plainly clear above, all that Sebastian Junger did was submit to the truth (advice?) of Gabriel Garcia Marquez suggesting that every imagination has got a basis that links it to reality (life). However, instead of departing from reality to imagination, as Garcia Marquez advocated, Junger came back from what was supposed to make him soar to the extreme heights of imagination to pleasantly seek warmth in the lap of reality—the outcome being a renowned piece of work on the top of the bestselling list. To conclude, the most important lesson we can deduce from this, disregarding the experience of Sebastian Junger in specific, is that delicate writing worthy of being described as a creative piece of art is accomplishable either through primarily counting on imagination or on the pure truths about life as well.

# Jack of All Trades

In reply to the view of Abbas al-Aqqad[18] about the concept of favorability regarding storytelling and verse, Naguib Mahfouz wrote in the Egyptian magazine *Al-Risala*, 3 September 1945, Volume 635 (According to a Wiki resource): "Apparently there are other reasons to explain the noticeable domination of narrative fiction over all sorts of creative work. Perhaps the most eminent reason lies in what is now termed as the zeitgeist. Poetry has prevailed throughout the epochs when instincts and myths were the governing standards. Nowadays, the era of science, facts and industry inevitably needs a new art that can unite Man's passion for facts and their inherited eagerness for fantasy. Thus narrative fiction (storytelling) has taken the lead. So, if poetry is being left behind in the race of popularity, it is because it lacks some aspects that will make it adaptive to the new era. According, storytelling has turned out to be the poetry of the modern life."

The essay from which the above statement is extracted reveals that Naguib Mahfouz does not have any problem with expressing himself via this type of creative writing (the essay). It is also obvious when reading his essays in *Al-Ahram* newspaper half a century later; even though some critics suggested that those essays do not reflect the value of the novelist who, by that time, had gained much international esteem and fame. Naguib Mahfouz seemed to be devoted intellectually and emotionally to narrative fiction (story and novel) before the 1990s (perhaps long

---

[18] Abbas al-Aqqad (June 28, 1889–March 12, 1964) was an Egyptian journalist, poet, literary critic, and member of the Academy of the Arabic Language in Cairo. He is perceived to be a polymath since writings cover a broad spectrum, including poetry, criticism, Islamology, history, philosophy, politics, biography, science, and Arabic literature.

years or even decades before it). As a matter of fact, he generously (and somehow hastily) sent his essays whenever newspapers, including the prestigious *Al-Ahram*, sought the honor of publishing his words.

I do not believe Naguib Mahfouz has ever taken the essay into due consideration as an independent form of creative writing as much as the story and the novel. It cannot be even described as something that holds part of his concern for the sake of competition between literary arts such as poetry—especially given that we see him expressing, since the 1940s, his conviction about the absolute dominance of storytelling/ narration not only over existing writing genres but also over all the forms of creativity.

I should underline the idea that Naguib Mahfouz of the forties seemed to be a better essayist than Mahfouz of the eighties. Perhaps the motive behind his mastery of essay writing, the above example specifically, arose from his enthusiasm as a promising writer who kept seeking the art (right path) whereby glory can be guaranteed, following in the steps of Al-Aqqad. However, Naguib Mahfouz, as the example above might prove, did not write essays beyond what was necessary (either as a reactive response when he was a young writer, or as an honor when he was a celebrated author). That was apparently the opposite of the valued consideration that the other novelists have allotted to the essay through successive generations in Egypt and other Arab countries.

What interests us the most in the above-mentioned essay by Naguib Mahfouz (in *Al-Risala* magazine) is the following paragraph: "Another non-less-dangerous reason is the flexibility of the story and its ability to accommodate all purposes. And that makes it a suitable medium to express Human Life in its full meaning. Thereby, there is emotional story, poetic story, analytical story, philosophical story, science story, political story, and social story. So perhaps the comprehensiveness of expression is more trustworthy than the two standards suggested by the great professor [what Al-Aqqad termed standards of medium and outcome]. It is plainly advocating that storytelling/narrative fiction is the most masterful literary art which the human imagination has ever created throughout all the epochs of Man's existence on Earth."

Naguib Mahfouz's tone in the above statement comes with

an ecstasy of victory and zeal for the new art that has invaded the "markets." But what is strange is that the debate about the issue (the Era of the Novel) has been alive for more than seventy years now. It means that poetry, the novel's obstinate rival, is actually more stubborn and too deep within the life of Arabs to be easily eliminated by a "new literary fashion," a trend whose supporters thought would sooner or later overthrow its rival (namely poetry) with an unavoidable death blow. But what happened is that the novel, though widely spread, is still tottering in attempts to find some weakness in (the body of) verse so as to unseat it once and forever from the ethereal status it occupies in the consciousness of Arabs.

What about the claim that the story is compatibly flexible to fit all (literary) purposes? Poetry also can respond to all potential subjects: love, elegy, praise, pride, etc. If comprehensiveness (of subjects) matters, then it is possible for Arabs to retain the old lyric form and redefine poetry not by creating a new form, but reverting to how it used to be centuries ago, through reinforcing its comprehensive aspect that could incorporate even the histrionic ends. Thus, comprehensiveness is not a new invention attributed to the story as a unique and unprecedented literary phenomenon.

Besides, the ability to assimilate all the subjects (love, praise, etc.) is not considered a supreme value in itself. What matters most are the depth and the appeal of expression in the identified subject. And probably it is acceptable to claim the importance of having an emotional story, detective story, and social story, but some zealous devotees of the novel go to the extent of believing that one novel can accommodate all those purposes and more. And that has to be a defective exaggeration. One novel that contains all types that people long for as a portrait of life will be like a "literary cocktail," something like a dish served hastily after gathering different foods and drinks to satisfy all tastes. But when that cocktail is compared to an "open buffet," patrons will pick what they like without having to randomly fill their hands with whatever is available on the tables. The case is identical despite what may seem for some people as a tasteless comparison between the pleasure of food and the reading/assessment of literary pieces of work.

As far as cinema is concerned, some may even relate this "cocktail" philosophy to make the so-called Seventh Art not only able to cover all the subjects cinema can tackle, but all of the arts as well. It is such a daring one-upmanship with little beautiful creativity, but not enough to prove that cinema is the most dexterous art that humans have ever produced. It is not even enough to prove that it has absolute sovereignty over all the creative forms as Naguib Mahfouz did when advocating narrative fiction. The peak of what will come out from that daring one-upmanship in appreciating the value of cinema is a new form of "cocktail" for humans—a cocktail that endeavors to suppress all the existing forms of creativity through mixing and inserting them into its own plans of domination.

The value and the pleasure of any artistic or literary genre do come from their unique distinctiveness, not from taking all the light on the stage through pushing the other arts to the dark corners.

If the artistic/literary value depended on the ability to accommodate all the subjects or all the different literary genres in one crucible, I would not hesitate to nominate the essay as the master of all categories of literature. However, I will not do it due to a number of reasons. Above all, I do not want my charmer, the essay, to end as a new form of a literary "cocktail" awaiting eager "consumers" who would love to try new tastes.

# A Gift from Al-Aqqad

Relating to literature, in the Arab world at least, it seems that people were bolder in expressing their points of view seventy years ago than they are nowadays. What we showed earlier about the reaction of the "young" writer Naguib Mahfouz in 1945 to Abbas Al-Aqqad through the pages of *Al-Risala* includes very plain allusions. These allusions revealed Mahfouz's advocacy for the story was not less fervent than Al-Aqqad's affection for poetry. When I compare that with the rising debate about the invasion of the novel in the last decade, I find that the two opponents are more reserved (disciplined?) in expressing their opinion. Those who seek victory for the novel are repeatedly claiming they don't have any "negative" feelings toward poetry or any of the other arts. On the other hand, those who still believe in the ember of poetry or even the short story, for example, are defending their art with bashfulness. They actually confined their timid needs to just being given the chance for their art to appear; they considered it to be beautiful and useful but not as powerful a candidate for "bestselling" lists as the novel is. If not in an absolute way, it is at least in submission to the circumstances of this era. (We saw this in *Al-Risala* in the words of Naguib Mahfouz who claimed that the novel was the poetry of the modern life at that time, or even that the story had gained absolute control over all the existing creative forms.)

Being reasonable methodically and intellectually at debates is actually required, but it is not wise at all to declare submission in front of the dominance of a general tendency suggesting that another trend is worthy of being granted privilege and power. So, the controversy about "literary supremacy" has existed for ages, though it seems to have been more fervent and overt than it is now.

The debate/controversy of *Al-Risala* magazine about the preference between poetry and the story, which did not stop at the reply of Naguib Mahfouz, was triggered by Al-Aqqad's opinion at the beginning of his book *In My House*. We quote here a paragraph of an imaginary dialogue of Al-Aqqad with a friend of him wandering in his personal library: "Then he went wandering with his sight as a bird while he said: The shelves dedicated to containing stories are so small! I said: Yes, and I won't mind if they become even smaller; because I, very frankly, do not read a story when I can read a book or a collection of poems. And I don't think that the story is the best of what minds have ever produced. He said: How? Aren't there genius story writers and novelists similar to those who master poetry or any other literary art? I said: Indeed there are, but the genius fruits (of the tree of creativity) are of different levels anyway. And the novel may be more fertile and intuitive than the eloquent poets. But after all, the novel remains inferior to poetry and criticism, rhetoric and prose. I am going to give you an example likely to clarify the case: the garden that grows apple tree does not need more fertile soil than the garden that grows sycamore and shallots, but sycamore and shallots are not better than apple even if they may grow in a more fertile soil."

Apparently, that was not the first manifestation of controversy about the priority of literary genres at that time, but it seems to be the most prominent one and the most well directed, which is why we presented it here along with the replies it brought about. The same issue now being debated seems to lack a great deal of dauntlessness and directness.

I am interested that Abbas al-Aqqad does not only prioritize poetry over the story but also over criticism, rhetoric, and prose. I highly value this instance of intellectual audacity from the great Arab thinker. I thought myself to be top-notch in my objection to the novel through encouraging poetry and the essay to persist in the long race to the literary podium. It is now apparent that the game of literary genres has somehow changed its rules. The story used to be the winning party against poetry and "rhetoric prose"; but it is now the weak party facing "Mother Novel" (we saw earlier that the mother can somehow be the begotten of its offspring). Wikipedia states: "Starting from 1945, Naguib

Mahfouz began his writing of realism fiction that he kept throughout most of his novels including Alqahira Aljadida, Khan Alkhalili, and Zoqaq Almidaq." Even though his first novel was published more than five years earlier than his debate with Al-Aqqad, Mahfouz probably wrote his reply when he was a storyteller more than a novelist. We will see that novel supporters, running out of the logical arguments for preferring the novel, turn back to reformulate the defense that the case is not only about the novel but about all narrative forms.

In the midst of the absence of a persisting revolt against novel despotism, and despite the difference between the two eras, the points of view of Al-Aqqad—as seen in his book *In my House* and his following comments confirming his attitude toward the story on *Al-Risala*, and perhaps in other places—seem to me (I'm quoting from football this time) like a penalty gifted by the great thinker (referee). This gift can be useful, with double chances to score a goal against the devotees of the novel. But I would rather deliberately lose this rare free kick (existing throughout different generations, as we saw) for one simple reason: the great thinker started his campaign against the novel because he preferred poetry over it, while I commit my "friendly" campaign basically against despotism of the novel or of any other literary art. I am unconcerned with the question of which should prevail—a question probably having no definite answer. Literature has a unique ability to bestow an original flavor on all its genres, one that can't be tasted through beholding other genres, regardless of how dominant or widespread they are.

# From Mahfouz to Al-Aqqad to Ali Al-Wardi

In his 1957 book entitled *The Myth of Sublime Literature*, the Iraqi sociologist Ali Al-Wardi wrote, "Many Arabic literature historians tried to explain that Arab people's interest in poetry during the Pre-Islamic Era (*Aljahiliyah*) was due to geographical factors. Ahmed El Houfi, a professor at Dar Al-Ulum in Cairo, says: "Arabs are a poet nation . . . and the desert was of great role in flaring up this poetic tradition . . . there, the moon dawns smilingly and plainly, sending its silver lights upon the walking, the talking, and the wakeful people enchanting their hearts. Stars would sparkle movingly as if they were diamonds chanting whisperingly. All of this pushed Arabs of that remote time to shove off in expressing and revealing what was lying within their (crude) souls. Arabia is a land full of light where the sun casts its rays east to west. And light has a concrete effect on people's attributes more than on their bodies. Goethe once said intoning the words within him: I want light! I want light!"[19]

Al-Wardi directly reacted to the statement above using a sound sense of criticism: "Once I came across what El Houfi said in relation to Arabs' poetic potency and tradition, I really couldn't hold myself from laughing at such a pedantry. He is eulogizing the beauty of the desert; but he forgot what God has created elsewhere on this planet where wonderful settings also take the breaths. I wonder why people of Switzerland are not more poetic than the Arabs if nature is the reason

---

[19] The first legal edition of this book was published in Baghdad in 1957 and the second edition in London in 1994. The book is a collection of articles written by Dr. Ali Al-Wardi in response to the articles of Dr. Abdel Razzaq Mohieddin, Professor of Arabic Literature. The book deals with literature and poetry and some grammar criticism, in addition to criticism of the literature of the Sultan.

behind poeticness? There are many others like El Houfi. They can easily find reasons for social phenomena the way they like. You can even see them come up with resonant expressions and strut as if they have already reached the peak of knowledge. Indeed, they are neglecting the concerns of society while they are chanting the moonlights, the sparkle of stars and sun movement from east to west, as if the sun does not carry on its east-west journey in other parts of the world."

Al-Wardi then stated his thoughts about the spread of poetry among Arabs. The comment of Al-Wardi, with that bantering tone, can be summarized in one sentence: The beauty of the desert cannot be the cardinal reason for the Arabs' love of poetry and their excellence in it. That's because every part of the world (Switzerland, for example) has its own original beauty. Perhaps the most eminent conclusion we can take from El Houfi's (unique) discovery is that most of the scholars are attempting to interpret literary phenomena; they cannot rest until they come up with an explanation, even if it is made through twisting logic to squeeze out any potential commentary.

For Al-Wardi, the importance and peculiarity of poetry for the ancient Arabs lies in this statement: "Poetry was the most important, perhaps the only, creative activity for Arabs. The reason behind this is that they were travelling continuously. Besides, they were obliged not to carry heavy luggage during their voyages except for the most indispensable for their life in the desert. They did not know much about the arts of writing, or painting, or sculpture or music or any other type of creativity; because these arts need different and many tools while they couldn't carry them during their long wandering journeys across the desert. So poetry was the only affordable art for Bedouins to perform—rhythmic utterances easily memorized and told without being in need of anything but the unbridled eloquent tongue to dive in the sands of imagination (desert)."

If Ali Al-Wardi seemed focused on the social dimension of Arabic ancient poetry, it is because he is not glorifying Arabic verse of that time. We see that his attitude complies with the view of Professor Philip Khuri Hitti: "Poems in the Pre-Islam Era were powerful in terms of linguistic texture, alive with its overwhelming emotions, but it was as well feeble in terms of originality of ideas and of inspiring imagination.

Given to such defects, Arabic verse loses its value when translated to other languages." In turn, Al-Wardi stated, "I think that this statement contains some truth. In that pre-Islamic era, poets should not be perceived according to the position poets occupy within a civilized community; pre-Islamic poets were, above all, warriors."

Al-Wardi was daring (for the time) when expressing his opinions vis-à-vis social, intellectual, and literary issues. However, his points of view are not rooted in twisting logic, even though his words may be formed with some sharpness given the many enemies, both in doctrine and in reason, he was facing in midcentury Iraq.

Al-Wardi did not commit his thoughts, at least in his mentioned book, to valorize a certain literary purpose over another, despite the fact that his book contains more than thirty essays about various linguistic and literary issues. Even when he discusses "the concept of sublime literature," he presents ideas that make any genre of literature sublime from his own perspective, in addition to the opposing views of the contemporary men of letters: "They term it sublime because it is beyond people's perception."

The issue of "social class" and literature was among the main preoccupations of the long essay that Naguib Mahfouz wrote to counter Al-Aqqad in the Egyptian magazine *Al-Risala*, ten years earlier than Al-Wardi's book. However, Mahfouz and Al-Aqqad were trying to grant power to a genre at the expense of another, more than they were searching for what made both genres sublime.

Al-Aqqad, when summarizing his opinion about his granting privilege to poetry over storytelling, actually plays the role of violent critics against Al-Wardi. Such critics mainly base their critical model on strong emotions (not necessarily devaluing their intellectual status) during the assessment process. Naguib Mahfouz in turn did not stop at only defending narrative fiction through showing its vital importance; he went much further in revealing the supremacy of narration over verse to state that the story owns the absolute potency over all existing categories of art. Then he proceeded to explain that the reason for that absolute supremacy is what he termed "the zeitgeist." He did not hesitate to refer to the epochs of poetry as the epochs of "instincts and myths" versus "the era of science, facts, and industry," for which he distinguished the story as its undisputed master.

Al-Aqqad waged the war to support poetry, while Naguib Mahfouz replied that the story was the out-and-out master of all arts. So, the two reached extreme extents of bold statements, which Ali Al-Wardi has not reached with his rivals yet (Abdul Razzak Muhyiddin[20] as an example) in their ongoing battle lasting ten years so far. Still, the daring of breaking through every issue shouldn't be in any way the objective behind every literary dispute. Thereby, the grace of Al-Wardi's battle, the least daring one to set a preference between the genres, is that it was concerned with specifying the abstract meaning of "sublime literature," despite not being derived from an agreed-upon concept. This also should not necessarily be the main inclusion of every literary conflict.

---

[20] Dr. Abdul Razzaq Mohiuddin (1910–1983) is one of the modern Iraqi scholars and one of the first educators who contributed to the university education.

# Between Al-Aqqad and Mohamed Kotb

New ideas do not spread just because they are great. There must be some powerful minds to defend them. And it is very common to have an untrue idea become widespread and invade other concepts in the market of reason just because a prominent thinker (celebrity) decided to confront others through spreading and granting support. However, judgment on the truthfulness of ideas is not conclusive. In literature, as in other aspects of life, there are no such true and false routes. Instead, there are desired destinations and undesired ones. And in most cases, the attitude of people negatively changes toward this path or other when a destination is judged according to their natures and passions. So, every method of thinking and feeling should lead to fruitful outcomes if people resort to wisdom as a basic tool of investigation.

A thinker or a man of letters will not dare to oppose the above statement when it is said without naming a genre. But practically, it seems that all thinkers and men of letters are rigidly adamant, to differing extents, when it comes to assessing the fruits of their minds. Indeed, in this they resemble all craftsmen. Even scientists in their highly specialized laboratories may feel the same and may resort to the party that supports their trend for granting good judgment for their desired scientific finding. Or they may do so to eliminate rivals not because of lacking competence but just because of purely emotional motives.

The controversy of "what's the prevailing genre of this era?" will not reach any decisive conclusion if we are seeking an answer that satisfies everyone—an answer that includes a single genre based on a mere logical introduction. And controversy is not supposed to end up with a consensus of opinion among all people by simply accepting the result. Still, people's obsession with their devotion (practitioners and audience alike) will not end when such eliminating procedures are implemented to satisfy the appetite for victory of the desired genre or art. This way of judging becomes more inapplicable, especially in the time of intellectual shifts where people are not intellectually stable in regard to their beloved genres—swinging side to side under the winds (of change) coming from different directions and perspectives. Perhaps they may keep up with the wind of the opposing party while holding the breath of a genre dwelling within the public conscience for decades or centuries.

The points of view of the Egyptian thinker Abbas Al-Aqqad (preferring poetry, rhetoric, and prose over the story), which we have discussed in many of the above paragraphs, have triggered considerable reactions because of the status of Al-Aqqad himself along with his abilities in handling controversy. However, the fact that he vowed his preference for a genre and devalued another caused the flare-up, too. On the other side, followers of the debates following the publication of *In My House* see that the opponents of Al-Aqqad expressed their opinions wisely and peacefully compared to Al-Aqqad's intense replies. Still, in some of his replies, though he tried to explain what he meant by his judgment (issued without constraints) of preferring poetry, rhetoric, and prose over the story, the ill pride of the first opinion is still inundating him, such that he again sharply confirmed his first choice.

This time, the Egyptian writer Mohamed Kotb and Professor Ali El Ammari thwarted Al-Aqqad. Of course the name of the first is memorized in the minds of successive generations, unlike the second, whom Al-Aqqad used to address as "the virtuous scholar." Ali El Ammari—or "the virtuous scholar," as Al-Aqqad addressed him—was a teacher at Al-Azhar University.

In the Egyptian magazine *Al-Risala*, volume 635, Al-Aqqad starts his article with shedding more light on the example that he presented in his book about privileging poetry over narrative fiction. And this example is likely similar to the example of iron and gold. Then he concluded: "We preferred poetry over storytelling in the context of dealing with both of them in my book *In My House*. All that we have said is that poetry is more precious than the story; and that the incomings of fifty pages of sublime poetry is more abundant than the incomings of the same sum of pages of narration. So, it shouldn't be said (mostly referring to the comment of Mohamed Kotb) that the story is indispensable, and that poetry cannot be substitute for the story, and that extending and preamble are two necessities of explanation novelists (story writers) have no way into."

Al-Aqqad's logic whereby he summarizes his advocacy in favor of poetry over the story is flimsy. This is because it is known that he once censured through poetry and prose what he termed "the fairness of rhythms"; but he is now showing up that type he disapproved of in the types of fairness when he compares fifty pages of poetry to fifty pages of narration. What is more unfair is that he bases the comparison on the products of two completely different genres to be judged by "the rhythm" that governs the production of fifty pages within both of the two genres.

So, it is not strange if Kotb seems calmer and wiser in the following quote that he wrote to refute Al-Aqqad: "The story is a psychological study that is essential to understand the secrets of human selves. Storytelling can substitute for poetry, criticism, prose or even rhetoric; because it is in itself one of the elements that readers need." Kotb continued, replying to Al-Aqqad's attitude based on the gold and iron notion, portraying poetry and narration relatively: "Iron is a useful mineral for making machines and building houses. Gold or silver or any precious jewel cannot replace it; because it (iron) is simply one of the metals that we need in peace and war, industry and commerce."

The above words of Kotb are sagaciously formulated in reply to what Al-Aqqad stated. But Al-Aqqad, when defending his opinions, besides that one when starting the assault, did not stay helpless in the face of a comment, no matter how wise and true it was. Controversy (especially the intellectual one) relies mostly on the ability to tolerate different points of view based on the arguer's talents and abilities. It specifically needs patience when the arguer moves away from holding a logical stance, especially if the issue is listed under the category of "potentially having different interpretations." And indeed, every intellectual and literary issue is mostly included within this category.

Kotb proceeded with the same reasoning and quietness, even adding some gentleness toward Al-Aqqad when he said: "I have read *Sara* [a novel by Al-Aqqad] and got in touch with the poetic dimensions in Al-Diwan [a poetry school he founded with Ibrahim Al-Mazny and Abdel-Rahman Shokry]. It is good and sublime poetry. But I cannot say that it can substitute for reading *Sara*, or that *Sara* did not contain anything new about deep psychological introspection." Despite this, some critics claim that *Sara* does not fulfill all the standards of a good story or novel. Indeed, some see that this story of Al-Aqqad's is only a mere study or a long essay about psychology.

Al-Aqqad did not give up, even after that gentleness of Kotb, but he became more insistent to do what he had prohibited in "fairness of balances/scales." But this time, he increased the "scale": he raised the number to one thousand pages instead of fifty. "This is the camel and this is the cameleer," as we say in our national proverbs: "Bring me one thousand pages of a novel or many novels and take one thousand pages of sublime poetry; then check the readers' judgment about what they felt after reading both the poems and the stories."

Al-Aqqad, in his reply to El Ammari, followed the same method of insisting on the first opinion with a kind of deference toward the opponent. As for my opinion, I think all that resulted from Al-Aqqad's approach in his long essay is what he mentioned in the conclusion of his reply to Kotb. Actually, it can be described as a retreat even if it is not clearly stated, but simply clarified what his views meant in the beginning. Anyway, he insisted again on concluding his inexplicit retreat with the example of iron and gold: "In fact, I did not write what I had written about the story to nullify it or to prohibit writing it, or to negate that it is a reliable literary work for a talented writer, but I wrote that to say I get more poetry collections than stories for my bookshelves. I say once more that the story is not the only creative activity that is credited to writers. Besides, it is not the only fruit that literary faculty can produce, and that having it as a medium of psychological analysis or social reform does not make it a firmly fixed phenomenon to be embraced by all writers; and the peak of talk about it is the same as the peak of talk about gold and iron (as mentioned in the source): 'iron is useful in factories and houses, but it is not bought for the same price as gold in markets.'"

# An Early Justice Toward the Essay

It seems that it is wise to blame the essayists before blaming the critics and the readers if the former have felt inferiority complexes toward the other literary genres such as poetry, the story, the novel, the play, and others. It is most likely that essayists have really felt so. They feel that it is better for them if they could (perhaps even longing) become poets or novelists.

Indeed, claiming superiority for a particular profession is common. And it is also widespread among branches (specialties) within the same occupation. This is because people consider the income potential of the efforts required in that particular profession, and often because claiming superiority depends on the evaluation of the people regarding the difficulty of practicing a profession, or just the impression of people in general.

Interestingly, the battle (fever?) of superiority among the branches of the same profession or the same art is first waged by those who belong to this profession or art before the others (outsiders) join the dispute. Some who belong to a given branch may endorse the idea of undermining what they are exercising (profession or art) when it is stated that it is inferior to the other branches; thus they become victims of the concept that some arts are superior under the influence of the reasons mentioned above or under the influence of any other stimuli.

For me, the idea of "infinite horizons," or "no limits," seems to be a standard equally applicable to all sorts of creativity and all other fields. In other words, I mean every sort of art is bottomless, but when practicing it just for living, then such level of difficulty/superiority could be applicable, while when the target is absolute creativity, then no standard classification (among all different fields) could be applicable/

74

acceptable. Therefore, I have no objection to the assertion that a given branch of the arts generally requires more effort than another branch of the arts, regardless of talent. However, when the competition is among art created with no limits, talent cannot be ignored and even participating in the race (with no limits) will be restricted to the gifted alone. So, those who simply say that a writer can be a genius in storytelling in the same way as in poetry are like those who say that the infinite horizons of the story are closer than the infinite horizons of poetry, and this cannot logically be accepted before being considered through specialized analysis.

Antecedence in terms of emergence does not apparently have a significant effect on raising the value of an art branch over another. But the antecedence in terms of steadiness in the process of establishing that particular art has an effect among people in the sense that they regard that sort of creativity as the origin of all arts. Accordingly, some people's consideration of which art is the antecedent (for example: is it the novel or the essay?) is of no use. Reasonably, besides the difficulty of determining what makes a completely perfect novel or essay, people see the history of events differently, even for the events that are not so long ago. In short, the most important thing is that the antecedent literary art is the history of sciences, as a whole, and the history of literature and arts in specific. So, counting on the issue of antecedence to judge the perfectness and supremacy of a given genre cannot be a precise criterion.

Still, when talking about antecedence, we can say that new genres have their supremacy just as old genres have their charm. It is most common that an art or a branch of some creative activity swiftly spreads because it is a new vogue in literature or art, so people passionately and eagerly appreciate it under the concept of "fashion of the time" . . . *but for* not more than that. And just as revering the old genre just because it is (historically) old is a mere invented process that does not logically fit, worshiping the new genre just because it is new is also an invented act that is not logical. In reality, both (defective) approaches/processes are being performed. People, practitioners, and the general public may resort to arguments; still, they mostly hold a specific stance either because they are yearning for the past or because of looking forward to modernity. As a result, the supremacy of a given art or genre remains confined within a set of factors far from the practitioners' excellence or creative talents.

Among Arabic literary arts, poetry has held absolute or semi-absolute supremacy for centuries. Poetry was not rivaled by any prose genre, which incorporated all unrhymed literary genres in limited forms. The story, or even the novel or the play, saw light only few centuries ago. As for the spread of the novel and story to the extent of seriously competing with poetry in occupying the hearts of Arabs, it did not happen until about few decades ago. If indications of threatening the throne of poetry have intensified during the last quarter of the previous century, the seizure of literary supremacy within the souls of Arabs by the novel in specific (not all narrative genres) has been mostly a recent event of less than ten years ago.

In the same way, the essay remained till the present time an influential art that no one dared to introduce as capable of holding supremacy without leaning on poetry or on narrative fiction. Actually, there are writers and readers who prefer poetry and essays over the story and the novel (as we saw previously with Abbas Al-Aqqad). There are others who do not like poetry and instead resort to the essay form of prose (social or political) but cannot totally prioritize it over narratives.

So, having a man of letters writing explicitly and appreciatively about the essay half a century ago is an event that deserves mentioning and praise even if the notice was transitory (that is to say, it occurred within the details of another issue). The Egyptian scholar Salah Zihni in his essay in *Al-Risala* meant to only criticize the critical comments of Mohamed Kotb about the two essays on narrative fiction he published in the same magazine about the two Egyptian writers Mahmoud Taymour and Naguib Mahfouz.

Zihni stated: "I was surprised and I commiserated with Mr. Kotb turning around Taymour so he exhausted the man and himself too. If he had known while he was rolling around Taymour that he also inserted three others in fields which are not theirs, he would have preferred to give himself some rest even if no one reacted to him. Hasn't he inserted Tawfiq al-Hakim as a man of storytelling while the latter has no hand in it, nor was he a school leader in the field of story? Hasn't he inserted Professor Elmazni as a story writer? With due respect that I, and many others, have for Almazni, none dared to say that he has an independent school in the art of story writing." Then he continued: "The second one is our issue here. The most interesting thing is that Mr. Zihni was not concerned with details between the genres such as the short story, the novel, the essay. But he was mainly concerned with precise classification of these genres based on the (literary) output of the writers he mentioned."

Without going back to the two essays by Mr. Kotb and Salah Zihni, classification of theories, schools, or literary groups is an issue that clearly brings up disagreement. What is important here is not who is the right one of the two, Mr. Kotb or Salah Zihni. (It is worth mentioning that the list of Almazni's work, which some publishers put in the list of his books lately republished, include writings that some consider as essays and ones that some consider as narrative fiction.)

The most important part of Zihni's suggestion is that he is talking with great literary respect for Almazni despite (?) his insistence of inserting him in only the category of essayists. That's an action that seems trivial to someone like me, but it is also difficult to find someone to consider this action nowadays; not for doubting Almazni's contribution to Arabic literature during that era, but due to disregarding the value of the essay in the present time as a totally independent genre. It means ignoring the fact that the essay can walk side by side with poetry and the novel and perhaps exceed them if circumstances allow. By circumstances, we mean those similar to the ones that made the novel overtake poetry and caused poetry to fall from its deep-rooted throne in the conscience of Arabs . . . so why not?

# Just Come in! The Gate of the Novel Is Wide Open for Sin

We previously mentioned that the route to composing a successful (widespread) novel is guaranteed through tackling contentious issues (taboos, for example). That swift spread will be attained through writing about all that is arousing, preferably sexual relations that take place outside their legal and social norms that regulate life within the relevant society. When sex outside the conventional institutions (namely marriage) is not counted as socially, morally, or religiously an odd behavior in a certain society, novelists (males and females) find another shortcut for marketing their novel through writing in the most explicit manner (obscenely?) about the most forbidden sexual affairs, like incest. This way, in the course of having fiction literary work widely spread by means of such acts, the matter seems to be a race to break through societal taboos more than being a race of literary genres (in the sense of aesthetic competition).

Because the race for popularity is apparently not bound by any constraints, there is no deterrent to jumping over two barriers at once. What we mean by jumping over two barriers at once is when a novelist (preferably a female) from a very conservative society writes about incest (for example) as a phenomenon that exists within her society, quoting a true incident with an alteration of names of people and places.

Perhaps it is not a problem when sexual arousal (no matter how obscene) is included in a novel that has a sublime literary value. The battle then will probably be at the margin of the novel as a work of art while, still, considering literary work as an influential tool within societies. Our matter of concern here will be about the artistically humble (aesthetically weak) literary work that gets pushed to the extremes of popularity only thanks to strumming sexual arousal (obscenity?). The latter, of course, is about to become the equalizer (provocative?) model to reach the furthest perspectives of (false) stardom.

Practically, it is impossible to ignore (the fact?) that literary success can only be achieved if the piece of work invades the audiences, and it is important to go one step back to understand what is meant by success. So, if success means that the literary product (narrative fiction) is artistically sublime, popularity will play a minor role in determining to what extent the piece in question will proceed. But if success means the potency of the literary work, and its ability to influence as many people as possible, popularity will then be a great measure of the successfulness of the literary fruit.

However, the issue is much more complex than the simple classification above. The dilemma (crisis) is when the judgment involves an artistically humble piece of work that is popular because of many other reasons, including the support from glamorous critics who believe that literature must break into the dark untouchable corners of human life. So, they do not object and even do not find any harm in popularizing a humble literary work that intrudes into what most prominent writers do not dare to approach.

Again, the matter is more complicated and more ambiguous, even after responding to the above categorization. The problem is that sexuality has become a factor in the popularity of a novel at the expense of another novel that does not include sex as a theme; the comparatively less popular narrative might be of more artistic and literary sublimity (or even uniqueness).

Actually, we are supposing that "novel fashion/trend" goes hand in hand with "sex fashion/trend," that sex with all its conventional (even though rarely) and forbidden forms is a powerful factor leading to popularity (and consequently to success!). We, on the other hand, do not accuse poetry, either in the modern era or the other eras when it reached the peak of lasciviousness, of the wrongdoings committed by contemporary novels. We do that for the simple reason (at least that's how we see it) that poetry at that time was not rivaling with any other genre; it was actually competing against itself. Nowadays, the novel is leaning on sexuality so as to gain celebrity over its literary rivals, even among works with the same sublime artistic value. Contemporary, and even traditional, poetry is to a high extent innocent of such (ill) deeds. In fact, poetry's dominance over Arabs was attributed mainly to artistic factors far away from other temptations such as sex. Besides, when some of the great poets of that time intruded into the forbidden areas of eroticism, they did it in few verses either separately or within one of their valueless/less popular poems. More explicitly, sex (both legal and forbidden) did not used to be a sound factor determining failure or popularity of a poem throughout the history of Arabic poetry, with few exceptions, as with the first poems of the Syrian poet Nizar Qabbani, before he shifted to devote his poems to women issues in general and not sex with woman/sex and woman.

Arabic poetry then remained more self-confident (I hope the expression will be acceptable) than what we saw in the novel. When the novel embraces sex as a "basic instinct" that exists in all fictional work (and sometimes cannot stand without it), we say that the problem does not depend on the genre itself but comes from exploiting sex as a basic instinct instead of many basic instincts that we mentioned previously—namely, fear, revenge, curiosity, and desire for possession.

Under the facts that we have shown above, it became harder for novel lovers to deny that their "beloved" is less confident—that is, because it counts on "external" factors (sex as a theme in one novel and not necessarily in every novel), rather than its own literary techniques and features, to reach audiences, compared to Arabic poetry throughout its different epochs.

In the West, sex is dealt with in almost every novel because it is a familiar detail in their daily lives being eyed with much directness, explicitness, and intimacy. The issue is different when it comes to our (Arab) societies. That's why sex in the Arabic novel in many (most?) cases is inserted or improvised. That's a losing cause unless its advocators count on the potential that the direction of influence is inversed—that is to say, reversing the system of social life where sexual arousing becomes part of the daily life of Arabs. In such a situation, no condemnation will be laid upon novel devotees on condition that, first, they stop popularizing a humble (tacky?) novel just because it breaks through the taboos of the society, and, second, they must be courageous enough to bow before Arabic poetry's sovereignty, which managed to obsess the hearts of Arabs for centuries counting greatly on its self-confidence without any need to hide behind sex or other transient arousals.

# Which One Is Hard to Write,
# the Novel or the Essay?

"What I feel towards writing depends totally on what I am working on. Now I am writing an essay about marriage. It is so tiresome. I feel that I am sitting on the black asphalt of a highway, writing insanely, while the eighteen-wheel-trucks are heading towards me fast; I can be crashed at any moment."

Then American writer Ann Patchett proceeds in *Why We Write*: "Narrative literature is different because when you are writing you are just trying to tell what happened. I always feel that I am looking askance at something very far during a blizzard trying to figure out what it is."

Ann Patchett is an American writer whose many popular novels have won various notable international prizes. She also writes essays in prestigious newspapers such as the *New York Times, Chicago Tribune, Boston Globe,* and others. Still, Ann Patchett perhaps cannot be the best one to answer the question posed in the title. Probably the most beautiful detail in the quote about the distinguished author is that she is not trying to answer the complicated question independently. She tried to answer it casually while talking about her experience as a writer. The most interesting point is that she showed the difficulty of writing in both areas without providing a definite answer, even from the perspective of her autobiography.

However, it is not a shortcoming when a writer tries to give a definite answer in this regard considering his own personal experience with writing. The problem starts when writers who align with one literary genre opt for judging other genres they did not experience (or tried and failed) describing them as easy to handle. Doing this, they grant their literary devotion complexity and subtleness—as if saying they are practitioners of some unique art that not everyone can deal with.

The most dangerous issue is when critics (no matter how artful) get involved in this mission: evaluating superiority among genres from the perspective of writing constraint(s). The danger here lies in the fact that people will consider the statements of critics as the most likely to definitely close the case—as if they were laboratory experts who analyzed the degree of difficulty between different genres through the most sophisticated devices of a "literary digital thermometer."

If a writer possesses enough daring to decisively state that it is more difficult to write in one genre than in another that he/she had practiced, it means the writer was lucky enough to run his pen (or his fingers on the keyboard) within the (easy) genre he/she aligned with faster than running his pen within the other (tough) genres.

Before expanding comments and analysis, we have to refer to what can be considered as facts in this context. The degree of difficulty cannot be the scale to measure the quality or the pleasing aspect of literature. So, if it is accepted that a genre is more difficult to handle than other genres, it does not mean the fruits of the more difficult one are more delicious and beneficial than the fruits of the other (light) genres. The matter here seems as if it always depends on relativity of judging the benefit and the pleasing aspects, either by readers or even by critics, no matter how some of them may talk about possessing the absolute judgments about everything within the literary context in people's life.

Ann Patchett somewhere else in the same book proceeds with her statements: "I really love writing essays. But now I am writing fewer ones because there are few magazines. I enjoy it but I can never sit down to write an essay if no one asked me to. I knew very earlier that I could earn as much money writing essays for magazines as when teaching. Writing for magazines is much easier." What is Patchett doing here? She is comparing writing essays and teaching. There is nothing wrong with it so far as I can see as long as the issue is related to the choice she had to make to get money and not for the absolute preference of the benefit and the pleasure of a particular literary genre over other genres. As a transient note in this context, I still insist on disagreeing with the English saying because the comparison shouldn't always be "apples to apples."

Ann Patchett turned again to comparing the essay to narrative literature. And I am not quite sure here if this will can be described as an apples-to-apples comparison. In the words of Patchett: "The non-narrative literature is totally different from the narrative one. If you are writing a book of 800 pages about the Chihuahua, you will need to make sure that no one else will compile a book about Chihuahuas before you do. And this is not an actual problem that novels face. Concerning the narrative literature, I have never sold a book before finishing it. I will never do. I write narrative literature in its wholeness for myself. I write the book I want to read. It is the story in my mind which I couldn't find in an existing book. The commercial success, or the expected commercial success, of a book has no power on me."

But Patchett (even after the above comparison between two apples) is still far from elaborating a definite stand, through her experience, about the difficulty of writing in the two genres at the level of writing technique itself, not about the financial benefits mostly based on conditions of the publishers and the market (of books).

David Baldacci in one of his statements in the same book (*Why We Write*) also went through comparing between two apples but in a direct manner, even if the second apple in Baldacci's comparison was the detective novel, not the essay. Baldacci wrote: "I will not be able to write a novel as a 'mystic option.' And I will not write a book that wins the Pulitzer Prize. I do not think that it is what I am doing, and that my talents lie here. Novels that win similar awards are characterized by depth. Both language and plot within it have the same power. . . . Can I spend five years of my life writing a book instead of writing a 'commercial novel' in seven or eight or ten months? I am not sure if I own the background and the talent to do so. The people who write narrative fiction are more organized. They spend years and years of their life on one project. This distinction between 'literary novels' and the 'commercial novels' is killing me. . . . I attended many writing events across the country and met many wonderful novelists who welcomed commercial fiction with big heart like I did. As if someone of them was telling me: Hello friend! But on the other side, I found much hostility. The commercial side complains: I write books of the same quality as yours but I don't win any prizes. And the literary side complains too: I write books better than yours but I don't sell any of them."

The statement of Baldacci reveals that the battle is not always between two different literary genres like the story and poetry or the novel and the essay (we mention the latter deliberately as in the title). War can be declared even among subgenres of the same literary genre, between "literary fiction" and "detective fiction" as David Baldacci mentioned.

Ray Bradbury says that he wrote *Fahrenheit 451* in nine days. It is a science fiction novel categorized as philosophical fiction. So it is not a "transient detective novel." Besides, many writers and artists swear that the best of their work took no notable effort from them. Thereby, the degree of writing difficulty does not seem to be a dependable scale to judge the quality and the value of a literary piece of work.

Because we are exposed to such an artificial analogy (conflict) between narrative fiction and the essay form, what really counts for me is confirming that the essay genre is able to accommodate, based on the talent of its writer, multiple expressive methods capable of creating deep insight along with pleasing subject matters. So it will be of no oddness for someone like me to eye the essay as a rival having more privilege than detective novels competing with literary fiction.

# No Market for the Short Story

"But I don't want to talk about Jonathan Culler and the approach of his book (Structuralist Poetics) in this context as I have already dealt with it in another distinctive area. My intention here is to draw attention to the first paragraphs that Culler started the sixth chapter of his book with; which I translated carefully (the paragraphs) to signal another opinion describing the era we are living in as the Era of the novel. And we can expand the description to make it the 'era of narration' to include the short story for which one of its writers (Alice Munro) won Nobel Prize in 2013. So she rehabilitated the short story genre which was not absent during the shifts throughout the era of the novel and its different versions that involve narration, namely cinema and soap operas. . . . So we can say that the era of narration is the era when poetry forfeited its traditional throne, after having been the most sublime literary genre for ages, to struggle in an unfair (to-be-or- not-be) war."

Thus the Egyptian critic Gaber Asfour retreated from his campaign of "the Era of the Novel," which is now widespread after it surpassed all the expectations of Arab contemporary literary audience(s). He actually (and in disguise) converted to the notion to "the Era of Narration" as discussed in his book *Narration in the Current Era*, which was released fifteen years after his book *The Era of the Novel*. It is not weird or inappropriate for a writer to question his stand toward a notion/idea or to reshape it to respond to new perspectives that might arise later. However, in this very context, we have two problems: The first one is that "the Era of the Novel" was unjust to all literary genres, not only poetry. When Asfour wanted to reconsider it, he engaged more players to the unfair team including the short story and perhaps more narrative visual arts. That of course was not against verse alone but

85

against all literary genres, like the essay with all its different types. The second problem lies in the fact that the first dictum started from a weird idea manifested in the results of Nobel Prize for literature, which novelists have dominated during the last decades. Updating the title of this era to "the Era of Narration" is also motivated by Western echoes, which Gaber Asfour plainly approached in his quote above. That odd influential echo is actually still holding its seat in the temple of the damned Nobel Prize. I am cursing the Nobel Prize for being the only literary background that has been regarded by Arabs as almost the only cultural/literary standard.

In the introduction to *Narration in the Current Era*, Gaber Asfour said: "Considering these new ideas, I didn't give up my belief that we are living in the novel's era. Rather, I opened new horizons to a new era of storytelling or narration, if we want to be idiomatically precise." He actually does not idiomatically term the expressions, but he goes toward more idiomatic generalization in attempt to keep his prophecy safe from any investigation. He did that through mobilizing more supporters by assuring more alliances, which military tactics/strategies necessitate in the midst of the battle, so that there will be no issue afterward with confronting (with relieved conscience) the supporters of other literary genres, specifically poetry, at least concerning the battle's title.

In one of his essays in the Egyptian magazine *Al-Ahram*, on December 13, 2004, Asfour confirmed that the era of the novel did not start with the novel *Zaynab* in the twentieth century "as many critics stated stemming from what Yahya Haqqi wrote during the dawn of the Egyptian story, which ultimately turned out to be the dawn of the Arabic story. The era of the Arabic novel is an ongoing process starting when the fundamental conditions of modernity/urbanization are fulfilled to incorporate all diverse languages and races and, consequently, reinforces a class struggle in which the middle class rise promisingly," Asfour wrote. Then he said, "And this means that the history of the Arabic novel goes back to the second half of the nineteenth century, when historical circumstances—social, political, economic and cultural—were vital for ushering in narrative fiction (novel) as an independent literary genre. That occurred in parallel with the waves of positive values enhanced by changes that had taken place during the eighteenth century, as Peter Gran confirmed in his book *Islamic Roots of Capitalism: Egypt, 1760–1840*."

There will be no serious problem, at least for me, when the issue is about the real start of the novel's era despite the fact that the dispute may have existed for more than fifty years with the contemporary Arabic novel, as we saw in the above quote by Gaber Asfour. Furthermore, a number of scholars, especially those who are obsessed with the roots of Arabic culture, believe that the inception of the Arabic novel was with Ibn al-Muqaffa, and Al-Jahiz in *Kalila wa Dimna* and *Al-Bukhala* respectively. Besides, in a more realistic way, (perhaps) they may even consider Ibn Tufayl's Ḥayy Ibn Yaqzan as a pioneering work in this respect. So, there will be no problem investigating the first straw in the nest of Arabic narrative fiction. But it is not that easy, or that wise, to claim we are living in the almost absolute era of the Arabic novel and that all that is coming (in terms of historical literary process) is mere periods dominated by narration. I do not hold this view for two reasons: The first reason, as some supporters may agree with me, consists of the less friendly feelings I have toward the novelistic genre (and narrative literature as a whole) than the feelings (of esteem) I have for the other genres such as the essay and poetry. The second reason is that I think prophecies (literary ones and other) are more applicable to fortune-tellers than to critics and academic scholars. Literature will be of no use if a given critic confirms victory/validity of a genre at the expense of another genre, even if that critic purports that he bases his conception on neutral readings of literature, history, politics, sociology, and many other fields of human knowledge.

In the book *Why We Write*, the African American writer Terry McMillan says: "I moved to New York and joined Harlem Writers Guild, something like EWU Library, but it was for black-skinned people. I read the story of 'Mama, Make Another Step' for them. . . . When I finished, the novelist Doris Jean Austin told me: this is not a short story darling, it's a novel. And everybody nodded. I did not actually know that there was no market for short stories. But they did. By the end of that meeting, I had already written my introductory chapter for my first novel ever, *Mama*." This incident was in the mideighties in the United States, the source of every possible contemporary "fashion" in writing (and in everything?). And after more than a quarter century later, I do not think that significant change has occurred in the U.S. concerning the market for the short story basically being dominated by long narrative fiction (the novel). Therefore, the retraction of Gaber Asfour by changing the expression "the Era of the Novel" into "the Era of Narration" was probably a retraction for the sake of precaution dictated by some transient (?) events in the market of literature, like when a short story writer was awarded the Nobel Prize.

Most likely, the situation for short story writers seems more dire than the situation for poets. The short story may, with a small alteration, become a novel, as we saw in the example of Terry McMillan. But not all writers of the short story can (or want to) make that alteration. Seeing that what is born from the womb of the art you are practicing is surpassing you to the horizons of glory is sure to provoke your ire, especially when the claim of literary supremacy is based on quality, not quantity/size. I claim here that it is possible, with some leniency in judgment, to describe the discrepancy between the short story and the novel as basically a matter of difference in quantity/size between the two narrative genres.

The matter then, as we have seen through the critics' comments and the experience of writers, is still related to the nature of the literary "trend," the spread of which is caused by many factors. These factors, when considered, seem to be similar to the motives that thrust any type of "fashion" into markets without considering their value as marketed products over others in the stores (markets) of literature and other stores in the daily life of consumers/audiences.

# The Age of the Soap Opera

We saw earlier that the prominent Egyptian novelist Naguib Mahfouz during the mid-1940s considered the novel to be the poetry of contemporary history. He even adorned it with absolute supremacy over all the creative writing genres. In the Arab literary scene, the prophecy of Naguib Mahfouz was late in being concretized if we believe that it was already the trend in the rest of the world. We state this with a note that Naguib Mahfouz did not utter his statement as a prophecy but, he believed, as a new reality that was actually realized in the world of literature and art.

What we have discussed about the Egyptian critic Gaber Asfour reveals that he basically did the opposite concerning judging our era from the perspective of a given literary genre having supremacy. Asfour felt a reality, then launched it after having reformulated it in a very summarizing title: a prophecy. But the so-discovered truth somehow got bogged down, so the prestigious critic corrected the dictum, changing "the Era of the Novel" into "the Era of Narration." In the midst of all this, poetry surprisingly remained steadily alive in the hearts of Arabs showing unwillingness to surrender to the hits of novelists and their supporters, who believed the hits would definitely knock verse down. But poetry surprised them every time, standing before the counting reached ten. It stood again and again to prove its appealing presence not necessarily in the peak of the Arab creative scene, but noticeably against other Arabic literary genres whose course of taking exclusive possession of (literary) supremacy is clearly fluctuating . . . in the Arab scene at least.

"What is the most dominant genre of the time?" This is a question that cannot be avoided easily. Those creative writing forms seemingly cannot live in the arena of literature without the supremacy of one genre over the other genres. And this is a problem of writers and their supporters—fans of literary arts. It does not exceptionally concern a given literary genre, especially since none of the rivaling categories is new to the literary arena in the Arab world.

As is the custom (the literary natural disposition) and as we showed above, the well-known TV drama writer Osama Anwar Okasha kept seeing (perhaps since the mid-1980s) that literature is living the era of TV drama. On a TV meeting in the mid-1990s (I believe it was on a Lebanese channel), Okasha advised his fellow novelists and story writers to turn to writing TV drama (soap operas) considering that written literature is retreating back against what is called visual (drama) literature.

Interestingly, considerable novelists and short story writers were affected by Okasha's prophecy. So, most of them remained unable to refute it with bold responses. When they are asked about the reasons behind holding to the novel or the short story instead of turning to TV drama, they answer that they can only find themselves in writing narrative fiction. This answer is so timid. However, a more daring/frank reply was made by a Syrian novelist on an Egyptian channel during the same era. The Syrian novelist stated that she does not have "the character" of writing a TV drama of thirty episodes. It is known that a scenario of thirty episodes if printed matches the size of few long novels. That's in addition to the fact that after signing the contract, the producers of TV dramas do not allow the writer to be inspired slowly, as the case must be with any novelist working on a new piece (which may take one full year or even years). Actually, "The next Ramadan"[21] is most of the time the ghost that is haunting all those who work in TV drama, not only its writers, to finish the work with ultimate speed regardless of whether the inspiration flows smoothly or not.

If Okasha's statement can be considered unrealistic at that time, his prophecy has at last come true, and its manifestations are still prospering under the fact that we are living in the era of TV drama,

---

[21] During the month of Ramadan, satellite channels in the Arab world are usually full of works of drama (especially soap operas) to be broadcasted exclusively in the sacred month.

but probably not in the way that the most Arab famous scenarist meant. Nowadays, the heroes of the proclaimed TV drama era are not the writers but the actors and the directors, and somehow the producers, too. There are other heroes/stars who work in related fields, namely set design, cinematography, wardrobe, editing, etc.

Accordingly, writing workshops (groups of writers working on TV series) emerged as the greatest threat to the individual writer's stardom. Writing within workshops is actually a Western innovation that made its way to the Arab world. Indeed, it is an idea that comes with some merits. Perhaps the most important one is richness of insight and inspiration every time the audience watches an episode. This is achieved either through having all writers participate in writing the episode or having every writer deal with one or more episodes in a way that not only refreshes the work but also entertains the viewers, who supposedly should not feel boredom no matter how many episodes they may follow.

Okasha was probably looking at these workshops when he expressed his irritation about the admiration foreign series receive from Arab viewers. Okasha did not get the chance to live in the era of Turkish drama which challenged the Arabic drama within Arabic satellites, with a lower professional writing level compared to American soap operas. Indeed, the Turkish drama managed to maintain its seat in the Arab scene even during intense political crises.

Unlike drama, narrative fiction is still resisting writing workshops except for shared work between two novelists as in some test cases. Luckily, story writers and novelists still enjoy the status of "individual star" when they address their work to the audience regardless of the role of critics and publishing houses in marketing/propagandizing the writer.

Novelists might be pleased when their works are turned into TV dramas or movies because they achieve more glory and have more to record in their biographies, but turning a successful literary work into a TV drama or a movie is not always safe for the writer. Literary pieces of work, when turned into visual scenes, may appear beautiful and even reach huge success, but not in a way that complies with the writers' thoughts and perspectives in the original literary product.

_Amr Muneer Dahab_

Could that be the reason why the American writer Sue Grafton refused, as stated in _Why We Write_, to sell the rights of her books to movie producers and threatened her children that she will haunt them if they do so after she dies?

# From an Essay to a Movie

Some of those who did not like the noisy debates following *The Clash of Civilizations and the Remaking of World Order* by Samuel P. Huntington around the mid-1990s—the book whose fame reached the furthest cultural horizons not only with the part concerned with political science—point out that it started as an essay which its writer "fattened up" when he saw the reactions it triggered, and then it evolved to become a book which occupied people's minds around the globe for a while.

Logically, a book with great traces such *The Clash of Civilizations* should not be disgraced because it evolved from an essay, for two reasons: First, the author himself was not born great but started with few books that had relatively modest influence; the author's first experience as a writer and as an academic scholar did not necessarily indicate his emergence as a greatly influential thinker within a few years. Confessing the greatness of a person does not necessitate having that person brought up great or born with lineaments of greatness. The second reason, the most important one in the context of the essay genre, is that the essay from which the book evolved is one of the literary arts. It is disgraced only because the lovers of literature (and its creative writers) prioritized a literary genre throughout long eras: poetry or the play, the story or the novel, etc. Additionally, people prioritized those genres over the essay, considering the latter to be a genre living on the margin of creative writing and sometimes totally outside literature, especially when it comes to criticism assessing literary genres that take, most of the time, the form of critical essays.

Disgracing a book because it has evolved from an essay resembles defaming a collection of poems because it evolved from a poem.

Extending the comparison range from what is mentioned above, it resembles defaming a man because he evolved from the child he used to be.

But for more preciseness in comparison, we should be aware that the essay is not a child within a huge book that contains a group of essays. The most precise consideration in this account is that a book consisting of mature essays is a tribe that contains a crowd of reliable, fully fledged men. Back to the closest example, an excellent/powerful poem is not a baby-child in the poet's collection, but a mature work standing next to other mature works, shoulder to shoulder.

Perhaps what has acted against the essay in the hearts of the public and specialists in the arena of literature and writing is the wideness of its form that accommodates all that pops up in everyone's mind, inking them on paper so that people can read. The essay then was so big-hearted that people underestimated it, unlike what they do with the other genres. Actually, they don't dare trying the other genres because it will be necessary for them to acquire dexterity in rhymes and mastery of narration techniques—skills comparatively out of reach.

In another essay, we stated that the greatest lesson of artistic ecstasy comes from looking forward to "infinity" without constraints. As for the essay in this context, its value mustn't be assessed based on the number of writers who dared to disgrace it, or, to soften the expression, with the number of those who accept that they coexist with it. Instead, essays should be evaluated by the ultimate artistic terminus where masters of essay writing, lovers of "nonstop races," lead eager readers to utmost destinations of artistic/literary value and pleasure.

The most eminent manifestation of disregarding the essay's positive effect on literature and thought in general is that writings and books of criticism, thought, and even academic studies in different areas (especially books that can be divided into chapters and sections) are in fact based on the essay, which can be shortened or prolonged according to the nature and objective of the writer, and according to the requirements of each chapter and section. In fact, no one cares, be it a critic or whoever, to name the art that accommodates all these writing genres, but instead they just refer to it as a book or as research. Actually, it must be confessed that much of literary criticism includes as much pleasure and usefulness as the literary piece of work being explored. Besides, a considerable percentage of essays that stem from books of great criticism and thought do not come only as a mere echo of literary work and life issues. Rather, these essays open new horizons for life and literature alike. This of course can be regarded as a subset of the point about the power of the essay form. In fact, criticism is most often an original instance of creativity that inspires and provokes other forms of writing, and this is one of the essay's forgotten merits/graces.

In the West, the situation is not that much better when we consider valuing literature based on the illusion of the hierarchy among different literary genres. As we saw in a previous discussion, the short story nowadays has no market in the U.S. compared to the novel. But the situation there is still relatively better in terms of regarding the essay as a literary genre contrasted to the situation in the Arab region. The problem in the Arab world emerges when considering the essay as being in the margin, not standing among the literary arts shoulder to shoulder, regardless of the flourishing "fashion" that makes a genre superior over other existing forms. Most shockingly, in most cases this supposed hierarchy is developed without regard for the artistic attributes of the pieces of work, unlike what the enthusiastic supporters of a prevailing literary "trend" throughout different eras think and claim.

We previously showed how producing a movie out of a novel makes novelists jubilant, and they are happy to include it as the most glorious achievement of their literary experience in their biographies. Regardless of the question of which one is more worthy of being applauded: the novel that is turned into a movie or the movie that derives from the novel (the question indeed needs much detailed analysis)—turning a novel into a movie is a testament to the success of the novel, whatever our attitude in answering the question of which genre should be considered the most sublime.

Thereby, the West deserves double appreciation for their valuing of the essay, considering that the latter can manage to inspire the cinema industry to turn an essay into a movie. This happened with the American author Susan Orlean and her essay "Life's Swell," which served as the basis for the movie *Blue Crush*.

95

# The Literal Followers of Western Literature

Our problem in the Arab world is keeping track of the steps of the West on all known roads. I am not certain here who is worthy of being applauded: "Is it the quickest one to imitate others or the tardiest?" I have mentioned previously in more than one place that some had denied the fact that Arabs were late even in knowing that they would like to be the subject of imitation. The sexual revolution in the West exploded in the sixties, and it did not enter the Arab world till after a full decade. As usual, it did not break through all people's lives, as happened in the West, but skirmished with Arab life through different media and cultural mediums. If it is easy to understand why imitation is so late considering sensitive and complex issues for Arabs like the sexual revolution, it is worth noticing that the situation/stance of Arabs in imitating (the West) is not much better (i.e., it comes late also) when it comes to other social, psychological, and doctrinal fields with less sensitivity/complex nature.

It is not fair to have imitation as an accusation of Arabs only. All Third World countries imitate the West in one way or another. As for the Second World, most of its countries have some original creativity. When they imitate the West, they actually do it to catch up with the first's advancement in a certain craft in preparation to surpass them while heading to new horizons of innovation. But the most appealing point here is that Western countries (namely the U.S. and Europe) are also imitating each other. It is righteous for the West to claim in front of the rest of the world (I hope the expression will be acceptable) that they are one harmonious creative "mass." It is a claim that won't have any considerable opposition, except when the battling is between two western countries, away from the rest of the world who will only watch, comment, and follow what the West's pure dispute may come out with.

Our imitation in the Arab scene is unable to come up with any parallel creative work or unique product in any field (I hope the absolute generalization is true here). We are often skillful in imitating in certain fields, but we stand there, just skillful in imitating, to keep wandering afterward in the vicious circle of the imitated work. And by means of modern tech, which has filled the entire world with its grace, we are no more than ten years behind the West in receiving a social or scientific invention. Maybe we should be more preservative when speaking of importing intellectual doctrines, as we are late when it comes to the deep understanding and digestion of such doctrines, and not only importing them to show off.

In the book *Questions of Criticism* by Jihad Fadel, thirty years ago, Jabra Ibrahim Jabra bemoaned the situation of Arabs in what resembled the subject matter we are dealing with here; but Jabra's disparagement was about literary criticism in specific: "Arab critics now are under the shock of cultural criticism. I start feeling this shock as a man who contributed, in my manner and in the manner of those who taught me, to the field of criticism during the last thirty years. This shock caused many of the critics and scholars a sort of stupor; they cannot understand what is going on in criticism's arena in France because of its having many names, many methods and many approaches, nor can they be satisfied with what they had taken from their teachers about approaches and methods of criticism. Therefore, we, or some of us, were obliged to say that there is no criticism (in our Arab world) because our critics are no more skillful in the French way to apply it on Arabic literature, while refusing to deploy the traditional way which they could have developed in connection with the special genius traits of the Arabic language, and with the Arab unique legacy. So, everyone fell between the two sides of the grinder."

Jabra continued his statement: "It seems to me that the issue became as if we are now being grinded between the two parts of the grinder. And the skillful one is who can get out of this dilemma through confronting the creative work being spread now in the Arab world in some way. If there is no such critical approach to this work, we will keep turning in the French modern criticism whirlpool which is not that much accepted worldwide as some may think. It is indeed still in the forms of schools represented by its individuals. When you now mention Roland Barthes,

Foucault, Derrida or Todorov, or others, we can only find those who always repeat that this is the method of Mr. so and Mr. so. This means that this method is in a personal way linked to the critic himself and not as a general method that can be made as a constitution or theory acceptable the way theories of Plato or Aristotle in matters of thought were accepted, for example."

The situation now is not very different after nearly a quarter of a century, either with criticism or other areas of thought. And what is most important to be considered from the words of the artful critic is that Arabs could have read their creative work by means of deriving from the ancient methods of Arabic criticism. And it is a favor worthy of consideration and whose return, after patiently spending time and effort on, would be more worthwhile than the expectations of the outcome of the pursuit of French critics' ideas/thoughts every time.

Nevertheless, Arabs not only no longer turn a blind eye to being stung in the same way twice, but also have become professional in the race to follow the West in different aspects, even when it comes to the idea of imitation in general.

With the novel, I will not say that the situation is only similar, but it is, as we can see, about to reach its peak concerning keeping track of the western literary and intellectual destination. And the fact that the imitation target this time is Europe in general, and not France specifically, changes nothing. That's because the European novel, as some see it, has been inspiring and dominating, even if I see that the U.S. is more dominating and inspiring in terms of regulating narrative fiction as the most sublime genre in a given era. That, of course, happens through spawning exceptional novelists or by the skill of making everyone appear more pompous in the international scene with their sense of creativity via the great American media machine. Thus, Uncle Sam has apparently become, with the novel and otherwise, the most attractive destination for the imitating Arab creators (and honestly also for non-Arabs).

In the end, I would like to go back to *Questions of Criticism* and quote Jihad Fadel: "Unfortunately, things are given (a new) life here (in the Arab World) after their lives are over somewhere else," and Ibrahim Jabra's reply would fit as, "And that's the catastrophe!"

# Novelists Are Cowards!

The saying "the translator is a traitor" is actually an injurious accusation when used in generalizations, but at the same time, it reflects some deep significance, with some reservations of course. For example, the translator is unintentionally a traitor when not able to convey the exact meaning from one language to another despite the considerable effort to honestly convey it. And he/she is intentionally a traitor when he/she conveys meaning liberally, trying to consider the specificities of each language and culture. This is because full literal matching between two languages or cultures is impossible by reasons of difference. All of this may occur when the translator has good intentions, but when the operation is conducted with less good-heartedness, the accusation of treason becomes overt with regard to the translator, with different details from one case to another.

By analogy to the above example, we can invent the expression "the novelist is a coward" as a project dictum perhaps in a way that bears wide interpretations without much embarrassment when it is injected within the market of literature.

The novelist is a coward because he/she hides behind an invented story to express his/her opinion. And by doing so, he does not show the audacity of the poet, who overtly lets out his opinions, making use of his own tongue rather than any other borrowed tongue. When the comparison is drawn between Arab lyric poets and novelists, the distance separating the two (the novelist and the poet) concerning daring in expression, each through his own means, reaches the extreme.

Most interestingly, the novelist does not hide behind one character only to say what he cannot articulate loudly. He instead mobilizes whatever he wants of characters to use their tongues/voices to express not only what he cannot overtly say, but what he lusts for in contradicted words and (deeds).

The novelist, of course, is not required to include an annex to his novel to state his reply or reflect his opinion concerning every word that his characters utter. On the other hand, we cannot deny the happiness that the novelist is immersed in thanks to the artistic nature of his work which bestows his ability to express all that is bubbling up in his chest; that of course happens with no need to be responsible for anything he says (and does). But after ensuring that the consequences are safe, he attributes the work to himself as a glorious achievement of antecedence in breaking through the taboos and deep-rooted beliefs within society.

In this context, the Arab lyric poet has the right to rest proudly in his matchless status. He has indeed endured the whips of modern critics claiming he is unable to shift from the traditional praise, satire, elegy, glory, and love. And perhaps it is time for him to be proud of being ready for all these subjects through his overtly expressed opinion, if the literary pride means plain expression of explicit opinions without any prevarication.

If the equivocation is about what the art is standing on, it has to do with its literary value and esthetic originality, not the fear of falling into the grip of a judicial authority of any kind. We can clearly see that equivocation in conveying meanings to serve for literary creativity was not an issue that undermined Arab lyric poetry in any way, nor a defect of its prominent poets. Instead, they should be proud as they have equivocated artistically and esthetically while loudly and bravely expressing their own opinions without resorting to any other tool of communication (characters), be it animal or human, as their counterparts among the professionals of old and contemporary narrative fiction have been doing.

On the other hand, if the Arab lyric poet made some moral mistakes throughout history—e.g., lying and being hypocritical—he at least had the courage to attribute that to himself because he did not speak those words via someone else's tongue. Then in return, he is afterward accused of expressing his personal opinion among the many themes included in his work; he is actually judged by the argument that overt expression of personal attitudes spoils the jubilance attributed to the work and closes the doors of potential interpretations that may hide what the writer tries to convey.

Storytelling practitioners, on the contrary, have also demonstrated a great deal of courage expressing themselves in public. But we have to be aware that their courage occurs mostly far from their work or in the margins (in a public event or a seminar about one of their works, for example). It is actually a noticeable habit that cannot be ignored when comparing novelists to poets, lyric poets specifically.

Accordingly, it seems that inserting personal views within the artistic/literary work is a unique trait/capacity about which we will not say that an artist or man of letters must not do, but we will say that it is the literary genre that cannot afford it in most cases. Thereby, this trait is worthy of more appreciation than it has been granted.

Actually, it is a common fact that a forensics report should not be influenced by the personal opinion of its writer. But I do not know how this generalization can be applied in a literary piece of work. The story, the play, and the novel have their own aesthetics for a variety of artistic reasons, none of which is the consideration of being entirely free from any personal interference on the part of writers. The opinions of authors are included anyway, but in a disguised way, as we have already stated. However, what is most important is that including a personal opinion of the writer in his literary work drives him plainly to bear it in all verses (in the case of vertical poems, for example), and that it cannot be considered as a defect in the work. In parallel, it is not a defect of other genres if not included except when the disagreement is about the boldness to express opinion overtly and not through disguises, and overtly through newspapers or during literary forums.

In this respect, when referring to the novelist in terms of speech boldness, the matter still seems ambiguous if the intended boldness means breaking through deep-rooted beliefs or exhibiting social taboos and not inserting new forms of expression in the structure of the literary work. It is logical to say a "daring novel," not a "daring novelist."

And if it is logically righteous for the lyric poet as discussed earlier to override the novel writer (and the writer of the story, the play, TV drama, etc.) when it comes to personal daring, then the champion of literary audacity is the writer of autobiography, especially when he talks about himself without any constraints.

Nevertheless, because daring alone is not enough to produce esthetically good literature, the most important aspect worthy of consideration in terms of tracking original literary work lies, above all, in the depiction of the theme with no prior claims (propaganda or other) of daring in tackling social taboos, even if the market temptations trigger the willingness to pursue those claims in this era or in another.

# Writing License

In the book *O Writers, Be Humble*, I have discussed "instruments of writing permit/license" which top critics are clinging to for authorizing a writer, not necessarily the best, as a glorious one while they neglect excellent ones just because they do not appreciate the way they write or do not like the writers themselves. We have stated that critics are only human, and it is not expected for them to evaluate people with perfect justice. And it will not be considered as strange when one of them is touched by an evil suggestion to bring down a glorious, kind-hearted writer due to mere personal (ill) desires.

I have also stated in the above-mentioned book what I termed the obligations of loyalty and obedience, as follows: "If the obligations of loyalty and obedience mean that the writer should waiver himself and should write in the way that critics desire, there may be probably three clauses as the following: The first is 'permissibility without disapproval.' This one occurs when the writer consents to the critic's provisions when the former realizes that the latter is right. The second is 'permissibility with disapproval.' This one occurs when the writer consents to the desire of the critic to satisfy the latter's arrogance and not because of pure critical provisions, be it right or false. The disapproval here is that the writer consents willingly to hand the steering wheel to someone else to direct his creative production even if the writer is still holding its details tight. The third case is when the critic who holds the instruments of permission insists that the writer stand by his stance to propagandize the types of creativity and writers that the critic desires and vice versa, not to praise any adversary even when there are some who are praiseworthy. Perhaps the most saddening here is when the writer finds himself unable to condemn when there is disqualified creative work within the side of 'the stamp holder,' the critic. And if the third case is morally common, then there will be no harm to ask the following question: Is it enough for critics to be only humans to have such sins forgiven?"

In this context, the answer for the last question is not our concern in the first place. The aspersions of negligence toward an artful writer seem to basically be related to people's customs throughout different eras and places. In brief, the meaning of this deed/custom is that popularity and praise are not always gained by the most skillful creators but are frequently gained by some less talented creators, and this happens for many reasons. And perhaps the closest reason here is that the most popular is the easiest and not necessarily the best. Or, in the best cases, the most popular is the easiest among the best ones.

Besides, there is also what we have mentioned earlier concerning popularity and praise as a result of following the compass of the heart (not reason) on the part of critics, the media, or readers. In this, they might be innocent of bad intentions to eliminate the best in favor of the less eligible according to the scale of creativity. To shorten the issue of bad intentions in marginalizing the artful/skillful writer in favor of the humble one, the term "premeditation" sounds more practical instead of "ill will." Every party has his own justification for his premeditation.

So what concerns us here is not the campaign about how the popularity of literary works disregards their artistic/creative levels. Our concern is the acclamation of this literary product based on its genre/formal identity. More specifically, we mean premeditation when (intentionally) helping the novel seize literary privilege/authority at the expense of other existing genres through incitation by its supporters who in turn have their motives in such bias.

With the widespread novel "fever" or "fashion" according to our recurrent previous description, the influential authoritarian power of the critics has become more tense (and provocatively irritating?). By means of their authority, they permit a "sect" in particular, while they neglect other versions of literary variations. Cultural media is also an easygoing provocative contributor besides the pliable, "innocently" obedient audiences.

Still, the worst of all concerning the novel becoming dominant in the current world of literature so that it's considered an "authority," which is enough to justify any literal existence and grant popularity, is that the circle of compliant drummers of the novel's fashion/supremacy/fever has become wider to include the authors themselves, including writers of non-narrative genres such as poetry and the essay. While novelists are overwhelmed with glee and pride seeing their literary genre adorned with that majestic crown, many non-novelists did not stop at the limits of surrender to the novel as a gracious and antecedent genre. Actually, they preferred stepping far from their genres, the ones that incurred wrath, to the most indulged one in the markets of literature, and all of them are waiting for the signal from the Master Critic: "Bless you, and welcome to the novel's altar."

# The Essay: A Question of Quantity and Quality

Back to the essay as an independent literary art, not necessarily to compare it with the other existing genres. Our aim is reading its deep potential literary influence. And if we reach the point of making certain that the essay genre has an active literary effect, we will not probably need much effort to prove its parallel influence on the real part of life similar to that of other genres attaining much public acceptance and prominence.

We have discussed earlier in this book that there were those who made some insinuations because the book *The Clash of Civilizations and the Remaking of World Order* by Samuel P. Huntington was originated from an essay that pleased people, so the writer decided to fatten it into a book, occupying people's minds worldwide. Still, I am insisting on the statement that having a book evolved from an essay is a sign of the greatness of the essay as a genre and not a demerit for the book that evolved from it.

But what would have happened if Huntington stopped his prophecy about the clash of civilizations at the limits of the essay? (Was that prophecy realized the way this man saw it?) The most appealing answer that deserves consideration is that the bounds of the concept would have been much more limited than the wide-open perspectives it achieved after the publication of the book. My intention then is not arguing about the book, which doubled the influence of the essay. But when we consider many essays, which have enriched the literary arenas and occupied their practitioners and readers, we can at least doubt that the original idea of *The Clash of Civilizations* wouldn't have had that considerable effect if it had stopped at the limits of that very essay.

We have cited many examples of great essays, which many books included. The most famous one in relation to the Arab arena is *Wahy Al-Qalam* (*Revelation of the Pen*) by Mustafa Sadiq ar-Rafi'i, besides the books of Ibrahim 'Abd al-Qadir al-Mazini such as *Qabdo AlReeh*, *Hasad Alhasheem*, and *Sondok Adonia*, let alone the book of Taha Hussein, *On Pre-Islamic Poetry*, which is actually a set of lectures (the lecture as the oral twin of the essay) collected in a book that (pre)occupied people's thinking.

That of course was at the level of the Arab (cultural/literary) world. In the same context, the Western arena showed more daring as usual where the essay makes its impact on its own without being included with others in a collection of essays, or being fattened into a book. The examples about this in the West are too lengthy to be listed briefly, but still we can note "The Death of the Author" by Roland Barthes as the most eminent Western essay in the literary world.

In the introduction to his book *The Author: The New Critical Idiom* (the translated version by Abu Dhabi Tourism & Culture Authority: Kalima), Andrew Bennett stated: "This book begins with a discussion of the two most influential essays on authorship in twentieth-century criticism, Barthes's 'The Death of the Author' and Foucault's 'What Is an Author?' (1969). In many aspects, these essays have dominated discussions of authorship throughout decades since their first publication: they have largely set the terms of the debate and have in equal measure been applauded for their radical reinterpretation of the concept."

We may thereby give another example about an essay causing literary revolution by Michel Foucault's "What Is an Author?" as Andrew Bennett signaled above. Nevertheless, the antecedence and popularity of "The Death of the Author" make us more occupied with Roland Barthes and his difference-making essay in this context.

The essay by Barthes consists of twenty-five hundred words approximately in seven nonlinked paragraphs, as Bennett stated reacting to the essay's criticism. Personally, this is what made me appreciate it more. The absence of methodical rigidity in the Barthes essay is a doubled testimony of supremacy of the essay as a literary genre, far from any academic recommendation that may pull it into the box of purely scientific research. It took "The Death of the Author" from between the university's narrow-spaced walls into a wider literary horizon. Somehow, this is applicable to Foucault's essay which is twice the size of Barthes's with more prudence in its methodical aspect. Still, respecting the methodical aspect did not put it in a better situation in terms of criticism, but it was criticized side by side with "The Death of the Author" with claims of their inconsistency, imprecision, and the inclusion of historical paradoxes, as Bennett noted.

About "The Death of the Author" specifically, and referring to the publication date of the essay in 1967, Bennett stated: "Since then the coffin of that essay was being scratched up and looted. . . . The Barthes' declaration has pushed this author's case to the forefront of criticism and literary theory. . . . Barthes' essay was considered as the last word being said about the author in the decades following its publication."

And if Bennett confirms the importance of "The Death of the Author" concerning its theme in specific and literary theory in general, what concerns us in turn from what is mentioned above is the supremacy of the essay's influence. We have visited Barthes's essay precisely to stress the confirmation that the depth of impact is not a matter of length even when compared to another valuable essay in the same conceptual area as Foucault's.

We have actually mentioned previously some Western matchless essays in terms of influence, such as Machiavelli's essays that his famous book *The Prince* included, and with more expansion the lectures/essays of Jean-Jacques Rousseau's "The Social Contract" and "Discourse on Inequality."

Here, as a summary, I can say that I feel no embarrassment to note that, except for the literary and artistic work that fall under poetry, story, the play, drama writing, and the like, it is applicable for other literary and critical writings in various sections of life to be described as belonging to the genre of the essay, besides the purely literary work that walk proudly in essay garb. Therefore, every book is about to enter the genre of the essay except the lies of poets (I say with a severe sense of guilt) and the myths of storytellers (and this one with rested conscience).

# The Poetry Lover Novelist and the Novel Lover Poet

Apparently, there is much in common between Tayeb Salih and Mahmoud Darwish despite the fact that they both write different literary genres while being subject to comparatively distinctive environments. It is a commonly held fact that there are differences between novel and verse. As for the childhood and youth of the two writers, both of them grew up in the countryside in totally Arabic-oriented environments. I deliberately mentioned Arabic in the second place here to show the differences between them. Because Arabic circumstances in the village where Tayeb Salih was brought up is mixed with African aspects as manifesting in the Sudanese environment; while the origin of Mahmoud Darwish near the Palestinian Galilee (whether Barwa or Jadeidi-Makr) retained the pure Arabic Oriental Levantine aspects, even though the origins of the place extends to civilizations prior to the Arabization process that following the entry of Islamic civilization to the region.

The two great men of letters, as far as I can trust my reading from a distance, share a sincerity and devotion toward the literary art they have committed themselves to, and to the cause of literature and art in general, and that is the most important in what follows.

Tayeb Saleh and Mahmoud Darwish are among the finest contemporary examples in Arabic literature of the "deep reconciliation" between literary genres—and I hope the expression in quotations marks is acceptable. The most beautiful of these reconciliations, which allowed us to describe it as deep/subtle, is that both writers love another literary genre a lot without having practiced it, i.e., as a recipient, not a producer. Thus, that reconciliation between literary genres can be described as instances of serenity and depth as well, on both their parts.

Darwish pointed out in a television interview that he would have wanted to be a story writer if he had not been a poet. I was actually surprised by this simplicity of expression when I first noticed (or perhaps before) my concern with what a writer may positively (or even negatively) feel toward a genre he does not practice, considering my attitude at the time toward genres other than classical Arabic poetry, which I considered to be the origin of all sorts of writing. But of course I was not "aggressive" to other forms of literature in what can be described as blatant hostility, but sufficing only with giving them "the negligence" they "deserve."

I liked that smart note made by Darwish about a quarter of a century ago even though he was not from the Arabic poetry school I hailed from. But the statement was, after all, the first of my attentive remarks, which took a long time before I realized the value or pleasure of summoning them to mind, such statements that can adorn literary genres with affinity and affection rather than adversity, avoidance, or caution.

I am indebted to Darwish for that. After that, when I started to deeply meditate on our Arabic literary genres in specific and their close/far relations with writers, my attention was noticeably attracted to the fact the man did not rush (quoting Nizar Qabbani in his famous allusions) to write a story or novel, but he was satisfied with enjoying reading narratives. Besides, Darwish did not show any embarrassment in confessing that he was hoping to write them when he answered a very traditional question: If you had not been a poet, what would you have liked to be?

So when Darwish writes nonpoetry, he makes "prose" accommodate the creativity he brings, being satisfied, along with his critics, with that sublime and elegant title (writing prose), and is far from resorting to the transient temptations of the novel and the story. And here, it is needless to say, but only as a reminder, that the literary genre model of prose arts involved here is the essay.

I will not say here "in contrast to Mahmoud Darwish," but I will use the expression "in parallel," with that example of reconciliation with the self as a start, then with the genres that are different from the practiced one. The approach/stance of Tayeb Salih is the same (i.e., similar to Darwish's stance) according to the order of my discovery (to both writers' stances), or perhaps according to a reversed order referring to birth date and the same experience of reconciliation in the stance (toward appreciating another genre) of the two great writers.

I believe that if Tayeb Salih is characterized by the most important trait in this context—concerning avoiding literary "haste" in experiencing other genres that he liked and the most popular ones at the time just for the sake of experiencing them—he was most daring in "proceeding with" the other genre that pleased him in terms of aesthetic taste and professional criticism. Indeed, his professional criticism was acknowledged by writers and critics alike, regardless of the fact that most of them are concerned more with mentioning the writers in fields that are more widely popular.

However, Dr. Hassan Abbashar Al-Tayeb stated on the cover of *The Introductions of Tayeb Salih (Mokadimaat Tayeb Salih)*, a book published by Dar Riyad Al Rayes: "In expressing his appreciation and valuing the creative introduction (Tayeb Salih's) which held the forefront pages of the collection 'Ghabat Al-Abnos,' our acknowledged scholar, Dr. Ihsan Abbas told me: That's how poetry criticism must be. This introduction is worthy of being an example in our subject. If it was all up to me, I would make it a course of literary criticism in all classes of Arabic for university students across all Arab countries." Through his appreciation of the creative novelist and describing him as a unique critic of classical Arabic poetry, Ihsan Abbas turns a blind eye to our accusation.

And if the introduction of Salah Ahmed Ibrahim's collection *Ghabat Al-Abnos* has in fact given that eulogy by a great critic such as Ihsan Abbas, the essays of Tayeb Salih that are collected in a book published also by Dar Riyad Al Rayes with the title *In the Company of Al-Mutanabi and His Companions (Fi Sohbat Almotanabbi wa Rifaqih)* deserve double eulogy as being deep thoughts on criticism of Arabic poetry, revealing the man's extensive encyclopedic readings, broad literary insight, and a very sharp critic spirit. He is actually a sharp critic because he does inspect his subject matters with an eagle eye, soaring high to bear down upon his target with full attention to the surrounding details, and at the same time embraces his topics passionately and with careful scrutiny.

Indeed, our literary arena is in great need of the culture of respect for and appreciation of different literary genres in the manner of Tayeb Salih and Mahmoud Darwish, the manner that can be described as "the culture of mutual respect/love despite creativity-related divergences."

# Between the Lies of Novelists
## and the Lies of Poets

"So when the poet owns deep insightful ideas without him knowing where they came from or their effects, the philosopher who can find himself in the same ideas only after a long meditation wonders in surprise: Who inspired this bedlamite with this abundant wisdom?"

Andrew Bennett in his book *The Author* quoted the above idea and words from the French writer Denis Diderot who, according to Bennett, summarizes through the above words "with ultimate dexterity the poet's ignorance of his work." All of this comes in the context of discussing theories related to literature writing and the role of the author in the writing process. It is worth noting that philosophers are not the only party mocking poets (according to Diderot's explanation), but they are joined by—perhaps those actually formulating explanations and theoretical grounds—a very considerable assemblage of critics.

In the same context, Bennett adds a quotation of Percy Bysshe Shelley defending poetry in his essay "A Defence of Poetry": "Poetry is the centre and the surrounding of knowledge . . . it does not submit to the powers of mind nor does it necessarily relate to the will and consciousness . . . and poets are truthfully the most amazed ones (by their own work) and they are bestowed with uniquely incomprehensible inspiration which they translate to perceivable/comprehensible artful words."

All of that was a comparison between the poet and other writers, basically philosophers and thinkers; but not novelists in specific, a literary title that had not yet been established and spread as a concept. It was specifically back to the beginning of the controversy about the concept of literary authorship, around the eighteenth century, as

Bennett stated in his book. The debate had its roots in an ancient controversy going back to Socrates and Plato.

In *The Author*, Bennett also inserted another quote by Plato from his dialogue *Ion*, when he states the words of Socrates: "The poets themselves do not pronounce these verses. . . . It is God himself who is talking to us through them." Bennett then comments on this statement: "This meaning-loaded description presents the poet as inspired by heavens, but he is for the same reason insane and ignorant, the fact that can be tracked and applied through the literary tradition to our contemporary history (of arts and literature). It seems that this description goes in two directions: first, it pushes the poet and portrays him as a marginalized person culturally and politically, culturally empty, ignorant and even insane. Second, the description shows the poet in some ovation as distinct from the rest, communicating with non-human supreme source(s) of wisdom, and disturbed with inspiration from God, strange in his society, but for all these reasons he can judge himself."

As for Plato himself, his decision to expel poets from his Republic is well known, and perhaps is the oldest, most famous, and worthiest of note, preceding everyone at that level of dealing with the strange idea and being brave/daring in that context. Plato explains his decision because of a simple and direct reason that poets are lying, and by briefly quoting Plato's opinion from Bennett, "histrionic poetry is unacceptable, because it distorts the minds of its audience(s)." The funniest here is Plato's argument that a real bed is merely a representation of the idea of bed, its sample, or form, and that "a picture of a bed or a poem about a bed is merely a representation of the former representation, and likewise the poet is twice away from truth/reality."

I would like to ask the readers for their pardon here for further quoting before we get to our whole point, which is the comparison among poetry, the novel, and the essay at the level of lying, whether in the way Plato discussed (with discontent) or in the way other people (pleasantly) expressed. Bennett continued his quotes of Plato: "The poet establishes a corrupt government system in the mind of people, through which the irrational side is magnified within its members . . . by creating invented images. . . . And it is tremendously far from the truth . . . poetry has a frightening capacity to distort people, even the good ones among them."

Then Bennett comments on Plato's words: "Plato's expulsion of poets from his virtuous city, just as his portrayal of them or the epic narrators in his book *Ion* as inspirational but also mindless people, has had a fervent, albeit controversial, impact on the concepts of authorship in the following European literary tradition, and on issues such as the author's sense (or lack) of responsibility, his moral sense or otherwise, his ability or inability to reveal the truth, seriousness or triviality of the tool he deploys, and his social/political attitudes."

We have now arrived at our bottom line, and we have presented the issue through many phases, sometimes different and sometimes similar in more than one place. The accusation that poetry and the poet is lying can be applied ten times wider on the novel and the novelist at the moral level. The novelist, through Plato's expression, is the founder of a government system who spreads extreme corruption in the minds of people by exaggerating the irrational side and creating imaginary (false) images. And, to further borrow from the great philosopher's sayings, it can be said that the novel has a horrifying ability to destroy good people.

For the purposes of argument, let's validate the moral influence of both poetry and narrative fiction from the "Platonic" perspective. And so from the same perspective, the essay genre should be glorified on an equal basis with philosophy itself because the essay does not rely on lying primarily. But still here, I would like to use a little dodging eloquence to account for the truth, and I hope that this logic may be permitted. So, the truth is that the essay can, as we have repeatedly pointed out, go along with the poem and the novel side by side, if provoked, in terms of its hidden technical abilities in the arts of description and narration.

As such, it can be said that the essay is "honest in nature" at the moral level, and in turn can be as aesthetically pleasing with lying as needed/demanded by (the) art, and this can be likened to the self-important reflection of many people with regard to exposing their vast experiences in life, seeing that they claim that they are able to be courteous with the polite people, while having enough effrontery to deal rudely with the impertinent people. This actually is the grace of the essay at the ethical level, which could please a philosopher like Plato, while persisting, at the same time, in its seduction to help those who love to fly in the worlds of fiction/lying spread their wings. In depth, it is adorned with the ability to combine two contradictions that are, most of the time, out of the reach of both poetry and narrative fiction.

# Fire and Thieves

In my book *O Writers, Be Humble*, there is an essay entitled "What If You Missed This Essay?" It reads: "your path of life shall not be changed and nothing will happen and everything goes as it is. Opposite of what the writer thinks, imagination is unlimited. The writer thinks that printers shall not work if the intended essay does not arrive and so it will impatiently wait for it. Such imagination is pathetic because the chief editors are in fact humans. They do not wait for an idea to arise from the book to make the publication of a newspaper belated. Such deed is wise in itself and it is not necessarily motivated by jealousy toward a well-known writer. And so is the routine that governs the life of people. Life continues even if the writer stops writing for good, let alone a daily or weekly essay. Even the sky shall not cry a tear if that writer stops living and goes out to another world."

That is a neutral (at least I believe it to be neutral) point of view. It's just simply to say that the writer is excused if he considers himself (like everyone) to be the center of this world. For that reason, quoting from my book mentioned above continues: "But what if the human being in general stays still in a situation of denying the idea that he is not immortal? What if he continues to think that he is living on the hope that he is immortal and that he is the only one? In this case he will think that he is writing forever or at least something bad will happen if he stops writing or if his life stopped after all."

Regarding the imagination of writers about the potential catastrophe if they stop writing or if one of their literary pieces isn't published: such imagination is worthy of support if the catastrophe is limited to the writer himself. But writers like to spread their traces on the whole world, and that's the point.

Even though I put into question that the writer himself will be demolished if one of his writings is stopped from being published due to a conspiracy or a setup, in that case the writer's fear about losing his work is logical and accepted, as long as we omit the exaggerations imposed by the writer about his universal importance.

In a statement for the book *Why We Write*, Catherine Harrison said: "Before the coming of the hard drives I was holding a copy of my writing wherever I went. I could not leave my house without it. I thought then that if my house is burned my writing (the real house where I live) shall survive."

In the opposite and during a statement in *The Rituals of Writing Among Novelists* by Abdennaser Eddaoud, the Lebanese novelist Hoda Barakat said: "Practically when we were running out from the house because of war, I wasn't thinking of the script of my novel. I used to forget it. The bags that we used to hold consisted of mainly indispensable stuff, especially the needs of my parents. From time to time and during the mayhem of war I doubted that the script would stay still. I leave it and I am not feeling sorry for it. . . . Life for me is more important. But during the last exodus my work was well developed, and I brought my novel with me."

In this respect, Barakat is different from the other writers who fear for their scripts. Even if life is more important, you rarely find someone who openly declares such truth, even if he is arrogantly describing the importance of (his route in) writing.

Barakat repeats in her statement that fact (which, itself, is simple, while being complex considering the daring of creative people to expose/declare it). She says elsewhere: "I write whenever and wherever I can, sometimes during pauses at work, or when my parents are not in need of my help. I work the whole day and I think my family is more important to me than writing; meaning that life is more important."

Because we are mockingly criticizing novelists in this book, we will not lack the evidence to prove that novelists are the most obsessed, among writers, with their belongings before their script is published. Novelists themselves would not deny that this is an honor for them. They justify their claim that their literary work requires more attention before the completion of a complex process (writing the novel) that

117

cannot be replaced in case it is lost or stolen. Poets, on the other hand, cannot feel the same since they have the ability to learn their poems by heart, so that they can reproduce them in case of any sudden losses of the original scripts.

In connection with such literary/artistic obsession, I remember a colleague whose fellows told me that he holds his "precious saving" in a bag that he holds wherever he goes, even if he is invited to a party or dinner with family. Obsession reached the level that this man held his bag between his legs during lunch, and if he wanted to wash his hands, he brought his bag to the toilet.

The weirdness of that man can be understood, considering the obsession of people for money. Most people consider the loss of money deserving of obsession much more than the loss of a unique novel or a wonderful collection of poems, so take it easy, dear writers.

# Women and the Novel

One cannot judge any kind of work without regard to the producer of that work first, assuming we know who's responsible for the work in question. Otherwise, if the author of the work is anonymous, we tend to imagine its source as we make a judgment based on that imagination. This can be true for every work in life whatsoever, not just literary works.

There are many stories being told (real or fictitious) of writings attributed to famous people, other than the real authors, and they were welcome with a great deal of admiration if they were attributed to real authors, or to those who are less famous. I remember one story (probably not real) in the opposite direction. It was claimed that the Egyptian writer and literary critic Taha Hussein, during a time when he was minister of education in Egypt, was disturbed by the rigor used by the teachers of Arabic while correcting composition. Hussein wrote an essay and told his staff to insert it between the essays of the students so as to see how the teacher would deal with it. The drama of the (made-up) story continued until we finally knew that Hussein's writing got a mark of 7 out of 10.

Not so far from the main theme, Al-Jahiz's quote supported the main theme; he said that some jokes never reached their humor without mentioning their creators. It was said that if some storytellers wanted their funny story to reach a wide audience, they would make its protagonist someone who is famous with humor among people. In this case the writer here is seeking fame through the easiest possible way: making it fake. Though the main idea is that judging literary works is something impossible and might surpass the author or the

119

protagonist, even in the case of an imaginary protagonist, as seen in the above paragraph.

Women are half of society, sometimes with a slight exaggerations in statistics (whether that is for her benefit, or for the benefit of men, in accordance with the place and time where the statistics are made, bearing in mind the difference in societies). But in literature, the percentage is so oppressive against women. (What about the different aspects of life when it comes to concrete contributions of women in social life, and not only abstract numbers?) Here we are not speaking of whether women are outnumbered by men or whether it is nature's law. Whatever, the specificity of feminine literature is a reality even before the rise of feminist theory in literature; we recall that it is a reality in the general framework since judging literary works is impossible without knowing the gender of its author. It is impossible for authors to come out of their bodies in order to create a literary work. The deep implementation of the Death of the Author for me lies in the possibility of opening far and precious horizons to read all that creation coming out from the author's unconscious outlook on human existence.

In his book *The Author*, Andrew Bennett suggests: "It is for this reason when we try to study the obvious ways by which men and women are represented in a literary work as of *Daniel Deronda*, we care more about the fact that George Eliot was not a man even if she was hidden under a pen name. For example: it's very important for Kate Millett in her prominent book *Sexual Politics* 1971 that the author of the controversial novel *Sons and Lovers* was a man who gated women. Would it be the same thing for structural criticism? Said Andrew in the context of exposing the feminist theory in the mentioned book, which was introduced by Millet for the sexual ideology of Lawrence, let us say that Davina Henrietta was the author. The point that Millet is trying to make is, by taking into consideration the social situation of that time, the novel of *Sons and Lovers* cannot be written by a woman."

It was possible that women might benefit from the concept of the Death of the Author if the absolute equality between the two sexes—in literature and life—was the ultimate goal. But that is impossible due to the nature of things, let alone that it is not the initial/original goal of the proponents of equality between the sexes.

It was logical that the theory of the Death of the Author goes against the peculiarity that feminist theory grants to women in literature. Bennett sees the following: "When it was like that . . . some critics recognize a specific determinism and a historical approach in the said attitude. Since the time feminist theory called for a literary tradition for women, critics declared the death of the author."

What is special in the relation of women with the novel apart from the other literary genres? In the Arab context, poetry was the pioneer in Arabs' souls. Even before the rise of ideas and modern theories such as the feminist theory and the Death of the Author, and due to the unchangeable nature of the Arab society in the past and in the present as well, the female poet used to be distinguished by her feminist poetry, and this distinguishing mark was blessed by her and her society as well.

I believe the most particular point is that the woman was a subject of poetry more than a (female) poet. And by the coming of the novel, this matter was portrayed clearly. Woman as a subject in the novel is more obvious and persuasive than the woman as a narrator or novelist. Of course this is not an underestimation of the female authors as much as it is a validation of the historical truth about women's effect on men and on life in principle. Even Eve—if she were to be compared superlatively with Adam—has the ultimate right of taking hold of drama in literature, as she has the right for existential privacy in life (I hope the expression is fitting). Adam is the absolute Human; whereas Eve shares with Man the general meaning of humanity, and then smartly maintains her particularity as a female (which lies in the opposite direction from struggling for equality between the sexes).

# The Invention of the Novelist and the Novel

In light of his analysis of the Death of the Author idea in his book *The Author*, Andrew Bennett suggests Michel Foucault's proposal: "the author is not a source of the text, but one of the ways in which he expresses himself, instead of spontaneously attributing discourse to an individual, the author arises through his relationship to the status of the text within a particular culture . . . we do not create a philosophical author as we do with the poet, just as it's been done in the eighteenth century. At that time it was impossible to create a novelist like we do today."

No matter what Michel Foucault proposes with that last quoted sentence, I am pleased to catch that quote in the context of considering the growing importance that people attribute to the novel today. Frankly, I want to draw the attention of devotees of narrative fiction to the fact that their lover (the novel) has not enjoyed literary prominence in the world of literature forever. It is not (by simple induction) a candidate for eternal presence as a queen crowned over the rest of literary genres, which are imagined by the fans of the novel to be scattered in the castle of literature in roles, ranging from princess to consultant to maiden.

Bennett says in the middle of his quote about Foucault: "The process of creating authorship responds to specific historical cultural determinants." I would like to comment on this statement only by emphasizing that these determinants are not only specific but highly peculiar, and therefore I repeat that if we wanted to make reference these days to the novel, it would be more accurate to say "novel fashion" and not "the Novel's Era."

The term "novel fashion" should not be taken as an indictment of that literary genre, unless the novel wants to be dominated by literary markets based on the fact that this is its long-awaited time to realize the truth that destiny of narrative fiction should take over in the world of literature.

The "novel fashion"—in the words of Bennett above, derived from Michel Foucault's earlier and deeper insight—means that historical cultural determinants (and, more specifically, social determinants) have pushed the novel to the top of the literary scene now, without being able to overthrow poetry specifically from Arab (literary and cultural) conscience.

Regarding "co-authorship," that can be read here as a context closely related to the idea of "the invention of a literary/artistic genre," which will be celebrated subsequently as a "fashion," says Bennett: "While cinema (movies) appeared at the beginning of the twentieth century as a new medium of creativity, it needed to develop its own myth to refer to its uniqueness and originality among the already existing flourishing writing and visual arts." Here we stand in front of a model case par excellence to form an image of art in the minds of people as desired by cultural decision makers, and again there is no problem in this. The problem appears only when people think that the appealing picture of huge overwhelming success is merely the logical outcome of a uniquely prominent and powerful art not only at the time when the model is created but also on the ongoing process of the same artistic/ literary tradition. The issue will be worse to the extent of becoming a cultural disaster if the said "critical lie" is believed by those who have deliberately introduced it. No excuses on the part of such critics can be accepted to repent for the sin of giving an illegal/unethical right for a literary genre to prevail over the rest of the creative writing forms.

There would be no harm in considering the novel as merely a literary invention that was made decades or even hundreds of years ago. From a critical point of view, there is no preference for the predecessor (creators), necessarily, but it would be ironic if some people were to dedicate a counter-argument to the subsequent instances of literature. It is like correcting an error by making another (worse) mistake equal in gravity and opposite in direction.

The scenes of literature should be the space of co-existence between all existing literary genres, the old ones and those yet to be invented by human imagination. Fairness requires that critics—and beyond them the cultural media—raise their hands from imposing guardianship on the minds and the hearts of the masses by turning their eyes to revering and honoring only one literary genre.

# Fame, Money, and Success

*The interviewer:* Do you think fame is devastating to the writer? If yes, then why?

*Gabriel Garcia Marquez:* Yes of course, because it is sweeping your private life. It takes your time you used to spend with friends, and your time you dedicate to writing. It tends also to separate you from the real world. The famous writer who wants to continue writing has to constantly defend himself against stardom. I do not like to say this because it is hard to believe, but I was hoping that my books would spread after my death, so I would not have to go through this long experience with fame. In my case, the only benefit I got from fame was my political advantage(s). Otherwise, I never feel comfortable. The problem is you cannot become famous throughout the day and you cannot say, "Well, I am not going to be famous until tomorrow" or press a button and say, "I will not be famous here or now."

Marquez's statement in an interview with Peter H. Stone was translated into Arabic by Mohamed Aldhaba in a book entitled *Date a Girl Who Loves Writing.* If Marquez himself did not correct/enhance his answer, I would say that it was merely an instance of self-esteem on the part of a superstar. Similarly, every artist (in whatever kind of artistic genre) keeps running in the steps of fame till he achieves it, making people run behind him, too; worst of all is when you see that the same eager artist gets bored (or even fed up) with a status he has been fervently seeking.

We all create, whatever one's field of creativity is, and we always have fame in mind as a tempting destination. I almost want to say that we all walk among people, even those who do not have any kind speech to address the masses, inhabited by a certain will for fame. I am almost sure that this madness can only escape someone who cannot confront people because of social phobia.

Although we accused him, Garcia Marquez is very well balanced in his complaint of the notion of fame. Stardom is often devoured by the creators, who generally deny that fame has a taste or that they were once longing for it. However, Garcia Marquez continues to depress the "balance" of fame during the same dialogue when asked: "Do you have things that you aspired to achieve or regretted during your career as a writer?" Although the question has nothing to do with fame, Garcia Marquez responds with the previous answer: "I think my answer is similar to the one I stated lately, they asked me a few days ago how much I wanted to win the Nobel Prize, but I think this would be disastrous for me, I would be absolutely interested in it, but to win it? Because the problem of fame will become more complex, the most regrettable in this life is that I don't have a daughter."

Because our research here is not primarily related to the ethics of writers and creators, what we are focusing on is the technical aspect of fame—that is, the aspect of the creative entitlement to fame from a purely artistic point of view. Although not a few ineligible creators have gained fame, and a great deal of it, original creators/artists are not always described either as famous or nonfamous—but, instead, the deserved quantity/amount of fame.

"The amount of due fame" is always controversial, and it is not entirely wrong that some evaluate the amount of fame achieved as being the deserved amount, since fame is not synonymous with artistic eligibility or success, though it is equivalent to what people like when (they notice that) some humble works reach fame regardless of any deserved critical success. It is obvious that the peak of fame everyone dreams of is the combination of the two achievements: high aesthetic value and overwhelming public renown. Gabriel Garcia Marquez mentioned above is one of the wonderful examples in this seemingly narrow section.

In the Arabic version of the book *Why We Write*, Mary Karr, an American writer and essayist, says: "Before I became a college professor, I ran a bar." She proceeds: "I had a very funny trade career in telecommunications. At the beginning of my break from drinking,

I was on duty as a magazine editor and I received payment. I started teaching while I was pregnant with my son, who is now twenty-five . . . I continued to write essays for the *Harvard Business Review.* This work did not develop my writing abilities but it enabled me to make a living— to keep breathing.

"I have not been able to pay the mortgage from the revenues of my books," Karr continues. "The myth that you get a lot of money when you publish a book is totally wrong, unless the book has a popular exceptional success. I have always told people that I am a poet if they ask me what I do, and that is what I have been telling them so far."

Although Garcia Marquez's relative balance in his statements about stardom is clearly marked by me, Karr seems more truthful and closer to the heart. I hope that I do not look here like someone who is not comparing—as the famous English saying goes—apples to apples. I would be satisfied if I am doing a further complex comparison between a famous apple and another less famous apple.

The question here is: Can we consider Mary Karr to be a successful writer, although she is far less well known than Gabriel Garcia Marquez? The answer—unlike Marquez—is that she is successful for the quality of what she has written, provided that we exclude commercial prosperity and materialistic returns from judgment. "No one really knows how to sell books, the whole style changes and no one knows how to make money from this work in any secure way," says Karr, without claiming— as we have just done—that she is a successful writer. She continues: "To publish a trivial book selling three million copies of a hardcover, and then you never show up again. All the energy and enthusiasm (at least from the part of publishers) are directed to those popular books for being most beneficial over a short period of time (in the market of books)."

In his book *The Author,* Andrew Bennett says: "In short, we can say that works (literary products) with commercial value were lacking aesthetic value. . . . The idea of the sublime literary work is that the work was aesthetically valuable because it was worth nothing on the material phase, this was a new idea during the eighteenth century. . . . In the eighteenth century, however, this authoritarian ideology dominated the institution of literature and began to define a particular concept of authorship," says Bennett. He continues: "Eagleton is mocking how the portrayal of art, the artist as an independent person, which emerged when 'the artist descended to a petty productive level of a commodity,' can be understood as being associated with some 'spiritual compensation' for the insult and humiliation felt by a person writing for getting paid. It is paradoxical that this puzzling concept of the author as above all commercial considerations, is precisely what makes his work capable for economic and commercial development."

How the eighteenth century was merciful to the aesthetically successful authors! But at the same time it was hard on the pockets of who were qualified—even within that category of authors—for commercial sweeping success.

Apart from my own personal interest, the novel was received at the expense of other literary genres and because of that extra interest in particular. Today's novel seems to be the literary genre that qualifies for the achievement of artistic and commercial success, but unfortunately it hardly stands up to achieve that equation, even with its most prominent writers (or both). In most cases, it tends to draw the scale of commercial success for the purpose of spreading. It was the strength of money and fame and commercial success at the expense of artistic/creative value and all that fall under the title of "literary success," a term capable of tickling the dreamy feelings of those unpopular original creators in any field of creativity.

# Beyond the Awards

"My happiest moments as a writer were when I won the Orange Prize for the novel, partially because I had lost it in the past against *The Sorcerer's Apprentice*. At the time of failure, I thought there was nothing wrong with it. It pleased me to have been nominated, and because Carol Shields won, but when you won, I thought, 'Oh, God, that's really better, it's more fun than losing.'"

That was the American novelist Anne Patchett in *Why We Write* expressing her feelings while winning a prestigious literary prize. As a woman she directed her feeling of winning that award and feeling lost in a previous experience. Patchett reveals sportsmanship at the loss and happiness by looking at the half-filled cup when she won the award, and then returned to believe that the ecstasy of victory is far beyond the pleasure of showing patience after failure.

Writers who rejected high literary prizes (Nobel as the most prestigious one) are well known, although they are few, and it was not for those who specifically thought that their rejection was in fact increasing their fame. There have been three. Two of them were famous before they rejected the award: the Irishman George Bernard Shaw and the Frenchman Jean-Paul Sartre. Shaw rejected it because, according to the expression attributed to him, "it is like a lifeline thrown to someone after reaching safe lands," meaning that the prize came late and he thought it would add nothing to his life. As for Sartre, his reasons are more determined in terms of the statements attributed to him; it appears he rejected the award so as not to become restricted by the award. Russia's lesser-known Boris Pasternak rejoiced at the announcement of his Nobel victory before the Soviet authorities exercised pressure and forced him to apologize for not accepting the award for his well-known novel, *Dr. Zhivago.* The Russians saw that the CIA had a great role in the high-profile writer of the novel and could serve their interests in the mayhem of the Cold War.

Who is the writer today that might dare to reject an award? This is a question for the purpose of censure/condemnation and not for seeking an answer, considering the) fluttering(reaction of writers toward awards.

Awards have become the section that writers—both famous and those who became famous by an award—put first in their autobiographies. Surprisingly, a writer who wins a prestigious literary award is not embarrassed to try for another award, and when he misses the prize a second time—as expected—he has no qualms about putting his candidacy for the second time next to his first win in his autobiography. There's no difference here between the author who has prepared his own biography or the one who got it prepared by others, and before that, there is no difference between the writer who submitted to the nomination for the award or the one being pushed or submitted a book on behalf of his nomination, considering that the author has the last command to ratify the nomination or reject it.

I am astonished—with such charm of literary prizes—by the fact that a distinguished writer is at the head of a committee for a prize, and then advances in a year ahead to win the same award. Such an act can be described as a craze for prizes.

The fever of prizes is more evident with the work of writers who have become quite famous (according to an official at the committee for a prestigious cultural award), trying a new literary genre to target winning the honor of being nominated for a prominent award. Needless to say, narrative fiction has become the best way to grab one of the numerous (valuable) awards that have been flourishingly created around the temple of the new crowned literary genre.

Al-Mutanabbi once appealed to the governor of the state (Sayf al-Dawla) more than a thousand years ago saying: "Award me if a poem is created to praise you / All the verses are mine though I pronounced none." The prize, while connoting that those poets around the governor were imitating his poems, was valuable because of the money it gave him and his family, and was never meant to have any literary value. It is difficult to argue that money is also the most important objective of today's awards, especially since each award includes at least a considerable amount of money, in addition to the consequent award of fame. Winning authors are largely advertised by the literary marketers in charge of the award as being pioneers of some unique aesthetic or ethical value.

It is not a shame that the name of a writer is among the candidates—in a long or short list—for an award whether submitted to the nomination on his own or put forward by others, and it is not a shame for a writer to win a prize, regardless of what is in the "back doors" of the award and regardless of any special mediations. It must be obvious that the winners are not the best among the competing writers. They just fit the measures of the award. Apart from that, as we have previously mentioned, there are conditions for the award usually referred to as "the general policy of the award," in addition to the "connections/intercession/mediations" imposed by personal motives.

However, both the most critical and the most innocent (at the same time) is the credibility of any prize at any time and place and the relative esteem of each member of the award committee, apart from any personal emotion in judgment, as much as anyone can claim to be fully cleansed of such emotions. The danger here is that what most members of the committee see as the best is not so, and therefore commendable works fall from the calculation simply because a reputable committee member saw that others are worthier to win. Thus, the dominance (which is purely of materialistic effect) goes to the prestigious authority of the prize to raise the stakes of a writer (and a small group of his colleagues in a short or long list), not at the expense of another writer but rather a group of writers who do not go hand in hand with the ideology of the supervisor of the award.

If it is not inevitable to obey the fever/madness of prizes, wouldn't it be just nice if each of us offered our own award for those who create without being obsessed with any award (either to win it and declare that on their autobiography, or to reject it for satisfying their ego/arrogance)? Of course we will avoid Pasternak who was obliged to refuse the award while his heart filled with grief at the loss of an award in spite of the fame he gained while he refused to receive the honor.

# Submissive Writers

I mentioned before that I rarely believe a writer who says that he doesn't like stardom. In a recent example, I had to consider Gabriel Garcia Marquez among those writers who I couldn't believe were annoyed by stardom. But with Garcia Marquez, the story seemed to be a little different. He was offended that he was so famous, even before he got the Nobel Prize. It would not be a great event if it ever came, but more importantly, Garcia Marquez looks like the ones who are less fond of our culture by exaggerating the ideals in general and claiming modesty. The man seems professional and immersed in his work to the point that we claim that it is sufficient, if not to distract him from fishing for the purpose of attracting more attention, at least to get him engaged in his heavy work and, consequently, avoid the claim of humility by any means whatsoever.

A few pages ago, we presented Jean-Paul Sartre, who rejected the Nobel Prize because the prestigious award (the ultimate fame and glory every writer dreams of) would bind him in an institutional framework. And Sartre here far exceeds Garcia Marquez in the place of freedom from the constraint of imposed stardom, even if he achieved stardom that he does not seek at all, only thanks to his original work.

But even Sartre does not seem completely free from the power of obedience to his product. Whether before or after his rejection of the Nobel Prize, his rejection embodied the peak of the amazing resistance to the power of the official institution, but this was certainly in favor of an informal institution that he could not absolutely get rid of. Sartre refused the Nobel Prize but did not reject the fame that was assigned to him before the prize, and even the fame of defending existentialism as a philosophy or the liberation of man constitutes a constraint difficult for the writer, even if some people imagine it is possible by moving from one principle to another or from one idea to another. Fame, in terms of its effect on a bewildered powerful creator, looks like a ghost that one can neither live with nor escape from.

Here the author becomes influential (as a less vocal expression of the famous writer) and is influenced by his audience at the same time, and perhaps influenced in general (by some other people/factors) more than being influential, regardless of his illusions imagining himself as a maker of public opinion and influential regarding the formation of the conscience of people. However, after fame in particular, the writer makes—whether he knows it or not—a public opinion that does not anger the public and forms the people's conscience, and rarely dares doing the opposite of that without monitoring carefully his audience's satisfaction and avoiding his fans' discontent.

The influential author gives himself the legitimacy to be subject to the authority of his audience by justifying the flexibility (flattery) that he should have to pass his ideas, which are not going to be absolutely his genuine ideas after reincarnating the audience's ideas.

In an essay in the *Sharjah Cultural Magazine*, January 2017, Wassini al-Araj says: "I saw with my eyes at some of the exhibitions writers sitting in a chair by the signature table. When you pass by their empty tables they look filled with anxiety and boredom. When the writer becomes a party to propaganda involving his community-based expertise, passion, religion and many sensibilities; he produces a text that people see themselves in, and he tries to convince his audience that he is interested in the product of his imagination. That solution is double standard and may detract from the prestige and value of the writer, as it turns him into a beggar of readability."

The idea of begging the reader, in addition to what Al-Araj wants to connote in the above quote, is a step toward the "cage of the audience" that the writer would like to sing from within his future literary pursuit if he wishes himself fame. But if he is already famous, begging readership will mean more stability and empowerment within the golden cage of the masses.

Amazingly, the drift behind the audience was not limited to an idea or a way of "marketing" it, but rather to the literary genre according to readers' desires/wishes, and this approach will be observed consequently by the writer to justify his manner in following what is considered satisfactory to his fans.

In the same essay, Al-Araj comments: "The time of the novel is necessarily not a matter of domination and race, but also a strong and visible presence at the expense of other forms. Today not everything that is sold is the best in the market, but the rule of vanity sometimes triumphs and becomes valuable: the writers of novels such as *Madame Bovary* by Gustave Flaubert in the nineteenth century, *In Search of Lost Time* by Marcel Proust, *Crime and Punishment* by Dostoevsky, as well as the novels of Claude Simon, those writers did not sell on the day of appearance more than a few hundred and perhaps less, but they remained references/models for humanity."

Al-Araj proceeds: "In the last book exhibitions that I attended this year, it seemed to me that it went out of the ordinary, much so that if one writer sells all these numbers in the press, I can say that the world is still a good place and that the writers can still live on their writings: these statements depend on what? What is the statistical observatory that confirms this? The statements of the publisher alone are not enough, because they are mostly based on propaganda rather than truth. Intense sales publicity does not turn the novel into Best Seller."

With the obsession of the writers described above, it becomes easy for the writer to describe himself as eager to be read by people. The terrible thing is that we see him pleading proliferation to the satisfaction of the masses, even by declaring fabricated numbers. At this point, the achievements of the writer will not stop at gaining the title of "beggar of readability," but he will be boosted to earn the title of "a beggar for audience guidance."

# Mass Media Standards

Writers get very cheerful when they take part in cultural festivities, such as book fairs. Apart from prominent names, writers don't dare to walk proudly in the book fair probably because they are suspicious about the intervening parties in the great meeting. It's supposed to be a place for hunting new opportunities. They walk in shame, fearful and suspicious about the publishers and the media alike.

Doesn't the writer seem to be a bridegroom who is not celebrated in his wedding as he's supposed to be? This is a question that cannot be answered negatively except for the stars of literature, who are not in need of a collective wedding/ceremony such as a book fair. Every one of them (stars of literature) goes proudly to all events he is invited to, and he gets worried only when he sees another star getting in his way. However, that is much easier than what a humble (non-star) writer experiences, as absolute ignorance is worse than stardom competition.

When literature has its own stardom and stars, it is a matter that should be welcomed with much joy and pride for every writer in this time, even those who are unknown. This may create a sense of hope in every newcomer to the arena of literature hoping to make great career as a writer. The problem lies in the way cultural media deal with the establishment of stars similar to that deployed by the advertisement industry. Creative writing, according to its job description, needs more skills and insight when it comes to determining the shape of the stardom of that writer or other. Maybe we were deceived by the fact that stardom takes importance only from the bright superficial side rather than the heart of it. This does not mean every star lacks depth; it's just that the bright is given much importance and more opportunities for appearance in the different prestigious festivities and cultural meetings.

So that's the way the media approach the categorization of every writer. Sebastian Junger said in *Why We Write,* "Media do this weird thing, if they decided that they liked you. They will create for you a surreal image that no one can reach. I am five feet and three inches, but when I met people they said: we thought you were six feet and six inches. What's in my book that made me look tall? If you have an amount of insecurity, that might give you more. That leads me to a more self-check. I was shrinking, I was depressed and my situation never changed to the better."

The critical point being not mentioned by Junger is what media would do if they don't like you? I will not mention the media measures being implemented on those who are out of the circle. I will just settle for the efficient weapon being used: ignorance. A known publisher told me once, how could it be wise not to make a media critic angry at you? Because he might turn a famous book in the market to something useless.

Sebastian Junger added in the same context: "If you are on the list of ranking of the *Times,* this is part of your job. There are wonderful books which never appeared in ranking while there are books full of stupid things being in the lucky list. Every writer knows that getting in the list is not related to the quality of the product at all."

Media figures of course will not remain silent about this accusation. The best answer they can provide is that the reader is the one who has the last word, whereas reality contradicts such statements. Media figures are the one who hold the list of what readers would choose and they are the ones who propose something that is already tested. There is also the cultural crime that media figures commit especially by surrendering to the power of the market and following the steps of their fellows in the advertisement industry.

In an interview from 1990 included in the book entitled *Questions of Criticism,* Jihad Fadel says in relation to our subject matter: "Octavio Bath, the famous Mexican poet, remained silent once when he visited Paris. He found that the voices of critics are much more than the voices of creators." Jabra Ibrahim Jabra replied, "that happens even in the forums of novels and novellas. You may not find writers, rather you find more critics making use of the glittering side of the media. I think that is normal because critics produce something that goes with the wave of media. Media can transmit the opinion of critic but cannot transmit the story of a writer, since the writer's job is to provide you with the whole story, whereas critics have power and dominance. They don't feel shame to express their opinions and critical stands, they may be harsh enough and their statements may create uproar. In this context, media tend to shed more light on the mission of critics who ultimately turn out to be the stars of the literary/cultural scenes rather than writers (the real producers of literary activity)."

What Jabra considered to be a normal thing doesn't seem like it is. If critics were once under the light of media a quarter of century ago, then lights are shined these days on the novelists specifically, to the extent that some critics are trying to become novelists in order to get a piece of the pie that novelists are already devouring.

The main point in Jabra's statement is that the basics by which the media operates are not objective. Mass media is concerned with the bright and media outlets are concerned with what they want to defuse, not what must be transmitted. Jabra states in this context that "many critics do not feel shame expressing what they see . . . and there are critics who might be aggressive that their opinion may create uproar that will attract the attention of media to transmit such opinions to the readers." Let us have a look at the key words: "shame," "aggressiveness," "uproar," which means that anyone who is "shy," "modest," "peaceful," no matter his/her artistic value, shall receive no other answer from the media than: "Absolute ignorance."

# Writing and Lobbies

"There are many white writers who earn big cash and they are among the best sellers, while their publishers keep supporting them, and they will continue to support them in all circumstances. Those writers tour the country getting big cashes just for speaking on meetings or gatherings. You won't find a black writer among them. It's racism simply," said Terry McMillan, the American novelist in *Why We Write*. It's clear from her tone that she belongs to the group of black writers whom she considers to be unlucky many times already.

Nagging became a phenomenon especially with Oscar and Grammy Awards due to racist attitudes. Such accusation is not pronounced only by black writers, but also supported by white writers.

That is almost similar to an era of total ignorance (middle ages?). White writers are not all against promoting black writers for the award. Nevertheless, the objection is likely to be less overt or hidden, showing up from time to time. However, the lobby we tend to deal with is not always a racist group, or rarely racist so to speak. The groups that take hold of the market of writing and control everything are groups from many backgrounds. It happened that I mentioned that in my book *O Writers, Be Humble* in the essay entitled "The Writer's Supporters," and I saw that the expression of "supporters" is more likely to be a light description compared to what is going on in the world of writing—a world full of all potential allies and enemies working on the same battlefields where not only writers take part.

I went on elaborating in my essay "The Writer's Supporters" that the term "group of supporters" can be taken as power/a political party/ an ideology/a literary or religious sect/tribe. . . . Because imagining a world without lobbies in every possible aspect of life is likely to be a legitimate dream. I went on saying that "every writer must have an attitude toward a group holding power (lobby) in case he is seeking fame and public recognition, since neutrality/justice/impartiality of the effects around the writer commenting on his work and guiding him is like a fairy tale or a myth in best cases. While the stream supporting art for art's sake is still a romantic dream tickling the imagination of a group of writers who are not fully impartial when it comes to valuating creativity away from any ideological effects. I guess that such writers may declare their war against their opponents against anyone who stands as a producer of art in response to merely a social obligation."

In case the writer is not willing to be put in the bright spots of the cultural and literary public, it would be safe for him to take a smooth attitude against any group, but for real, is there anyone who is not willing to be put in the lights? Some can trace the path of abnegation but without ignoring take the path to light and fame. I still cannot believe that some writers say that fame is not their concern. The bottom line is that the writer is writing to the masses and not himself. So, this judgment is illogical.

There is no harm in getting to the path of fame. But the main obstacle is how to get to the horizons of fame that are full of critical influential groups that a writer has to make use of to be safe. Skillful seekers of fame are the ones who know how to sympathize with more than a group; some of them may reach the level of setting enmity to only one group in a clear strategy to gain fame not only as a duty dictated by life circumstances.

As we have explained in our previous essay about "Mass Media Standards," our main goal is not to present media as an innocent entity given that it just transmits the war among the proclaimed "militias." If it is not mass media that should be the largest Mafia, it should at least regarded as the window that every Mafia opens to the public or perhaps a window where no writer can pass without being guided by a lobby.

Accordingly, every group must shove an alliance with the media so that the latter can reinforce their chances to get to the large masses. The media play a vital role in rendering a less prominent piece of work a subject of public debates.

The group as an entity seems to be a destiny for writers from the beginning of time. We can describe it as the clan in the pre-Islamic period or the fans of Jarir against Al-Farazdaq in the Umayyads Caliphate. Or maybe the supporters of Abu Firas against Al-Mutanabbi, or the ones who stand for Al-Aqqad against Ahmed Shawqi. Furthermore, we might consider them as the ones who stand for Taha Hussein against Mustafa Sadiq al-Rafii. We can sum up all and say that it is a literary sect fighting/struggling against other sects (having opted for some other approach or philosophy).

As I said before in *O Writers, Be Humble*, it is noteworthy to mention that if we imagine a utopia, but not in the sense of Plato, in which the power of groups does not exist in order to promote a writer, then a group of writers will gather and create power for themselves in order to destroy other groups.

Finally, it would not be wise to deny that writers are creating what they need of influential groups or support what they like out of the already existing groups in a life that is naturally full of lobbies.

# Not Every Interesting Book
# Is Necessarily a Novel

"I still believe that we are not really living the Era of narrative fiction especially with the absence of mechanisms of assessment, promotion, distribution and conception. It has been a time of retreat of the said novelistic privileged genre as it was the case with other literary genres (like Epic and other great classical genres) throughout the history of literature. There is something subtle taking place in the Novel's Castle. Even the Nobel Prize went out from its traditional approach to literature broadening it so as to include other parallel categories co-existing besides the novel such as lyrical text with Bob Dylan, in addition to the investigative/narrative/political journalistic reports. That means something is going on inside the body of the novel and tears its classical specificity and even its 'sanctity.' There are other types taking the lead in literature which doesn't have the characteristics of the novel as it was known, written and perceived before."

In an essay published in *Sharjah Magazine* in 2017, as mentioned above, Wassini al-Araj amazingly and interestingly dealt with the love both Tayeb Salih and Mahmoud Darwish used to have toward an art they did not perform since they saw it with the eye of a reader and not a creator. It is somehow similar to my notion about "between the novelist who adores verse and the poet who adores narrative fiction." Both Salih and Darwish are good examples of contemporary writers illustrating deep reconciliation between different literary genres, a model of (literary/artistic) reconciliation worthy of being described as an instance of "peace and insight."

Al-Araj exceeds what we termed "deep reconciliation" between Salih and Darwish to embrace some "comforting daring." He in fact did not only reveal his admiration for a different literary genre (from the one he is known for), but he also had the courage to stand against the slogan of the "Novel's Era" which is about to take the lead in Arab literature as an unquestionable postulate. He even greatly welcomed awarding the Nobel Prize to certain unconventional literary variant genres (some of which have been condemned even in the West). Furthermore, he confirmed his feeling of doubt in regard to the future of the novel's peculiarity and majesty.

However, Al-Araj's "comforting daring" did not stop there. It even pronounced the imminent death of the novel (besides the other forms of creative writing). In connection to his declaration above, he proceeds as follows: "narrative fiction being practiced/experimented by whoever want to 'write.' In fact the stigmatization of novel writing is not an instance of unique creativity, nor is it a part of a process of democratization of writing given to the literary 'products' being created lately. Instead, they are signs of the gradual fall of the novel till it will be paralyzed along with its effectiveness as an independent genre open to renovation and modernity. It's a new time coming to eradicate all sorts of written literary products, not only the novel, in the light of the flagrant domination of visual arts and social media which 'has stolen' every possible aspect of life and impact from classical/conventional literary genres, if these genres are not willing to accept the requirements of a surprisingly changing contexts where they live."

Al-Araj says that the novel is not that powerful candidate (it used to be) for the throne of literature arenas anymore, adding that all conventional written literary genres, too, are not capable of taking hold of the domination over the world of literature and over audiences. This is happening while social mass media keeps reinforcing the new "Visual Era."

David Baldacci was also concerned about the matter of the new trend in the eyes of modern circumstances that govern the work of the novelist. In *Why We Write*, the American novelist said "I cannot write a novel like *Sophie's World* and I will not write a book that can win the Pulitzer. I don't think that my talents exist in here. Novels winning such awards are deep, where the language and the story are going strong and subtle (hand in hand). Can I spend five years of my life writing one book rather than writing a 'commercial novel' (product) which might take only seven or eight or ten months? I am not sure whether I have the background and the talent to do that. Story writers are well organized; they spend years and years in one project. They can benefit from everything they have (skill and talent) to work on that very story."

Unlike Al-Araj, Baldacci doesn't seem to be patient and peaceful in front of his competitors in the field of "literary novels," which are full of deep insight as he describes. He keeps raising the question with a distressed tone: "This discrimination between commercial and literary novels is really killing me. It's like dividing one unity into two (different parties). Something like breaking the union between The American Federation of Labor *and* Congress *of* Industrial Organizations. Who will encourage this process? The big companies of course."

However, Baldacci keeps relating his experience, but more peacefully this time: "It happens that I went to many book-related gatherings in the every part of the country, I met many novelists who accept 'commercial' writers like me with open mind. As if some of them were telling me 'welcome, my comrade!' On the other hand, I found much enmity too. The 'commercial' party is complaining: I write good books just like yours, but I don't win any awards. While the literary party complains: I write books better than yours but I can never sell any."

In another attempt, Baldacci is trying to express his view, with some kind of objectivism though mixed with anger, insisting that his commercial novels are worthy of interest and success compared to their privileged literary counterparts, adding that "someone asked John Updike, why don't you write a mystery novel? He replied: I am not that smart. Updike wrote many wonderful books and won two Pulitzer Prizes but he's got different skills/talents. The same thing happens to me. I can never write *Rabbit, Run*. Writing mystery novels needs much planning and well-developed plot. It's like putting a bomb in page 4 and it will not explode until page 400. Even worse books require some talent to write them."

I was amazed once when I was at a book fair. A reader was insisting on buying one of my books (I was there for the book signing of that particular title) from other books that the publisher was trying to persuade him to get. Suddenly, I was shocked when I heard him saying: "I want just a light book that I can read before going to bed." The title of my book, unlike its content, had some of the ingredients the man was seeking.

The most important part of what happened in that incident is that I was wondering: Where is the harm if the book is a good one to be read before going to bed? This being a fact, it does not necessarily contradict the notion of deep insight in the literary piece of work being subject to such an approach from the part of similar readers like the one we have just mentioned.

I was also amazed by the fact that my reader was not looking for a novel to enjoy before falling asleep. He was looking for pleasure and satisfaction (or even beauty), far from considering it reachable only through a specific literary genre.

I respect David Baldacci's assumption about the pure value of commercial novel versus literary novel, even if he was arguing in favor of a particular category of literature rather than other distinct genres, without regard to his tone of doubt concerning the validity of what he is writing. I think that much consideration/esteem should go to those (readers or literary critics) looking for pleasure and knowledge away from the narrow "discrimination" among literary genres. The notion is openly expressed in the statement of Wassini al-Araj when he considers literature, the novel in specific, in constant need to attune itself in connection with the different changing contexts. Otherwise, there would be no other choice but leading to extinction.

# I Can Write This Way

"When I went to the college, I had had a good literary background. At the University of Bogota I started making friends to whom I am grateful for introducing me to a bunch of modern writers. One night, a friend of mine lent me a book of Franz Kafka. I went back to my room and I started reading 'The Metamorphosis.' I was shocked reading the first line. I was likely to fall from my bed. I was surprisingly amazed: 'as Gregor Samsa awoke one morning from uneasy dreams he found himself transformed in his bed into a gigantic insect-like creature.' When I read this line I thought for a moment and said: I don't know someone who was permitted to write this way. If I had known, I would have started writing long ago."

Thus, a well-known writer of the twentieth century described the way he discovered a role model writer—a path to follow in his literary pursuit/career. It might be surprising for many that Gabriel Garcia Marquez is the writer who said this. The majority of people think that writers are born with that skill/talent of writing which they must hold as an unenviable fate/burden for the rest of their lives.

In another part of the book *Date a Girl Who Loves Writing*, which is where the Garcia Marquez quote is from, the Japanese novelist Haruki Murakami presented a similar experience: "I can remember the moment exactly, it was half past one in the first days of April 1978. I was in Ginkgo Stadium watching baseball. The stadium was close to my flat. I was a fan of Yakut Swallows. It was a nice day of spring with a clear sky and warm air. When the match was being played, I got the idea: 'You know? I have to write a novel.' I still remember the open sky and me sitting on the grass, and the sound of the ball and the bat. Something fell from the sky, whatever it was, I received it for real."

Murakami proceeds: "I didn't have the motivation to be a novelist. I just had a deep desire to write a novel. I did not know what to write about. I had just the faith that I can write something convincing. When I sat at my desk for the first time, I realized that I did not even have a suitable pen. I went to the shop of Kinokuniya in Shinjuku; I bought papers and a pen with $5. It was a small budget to start with. During that fall, I end up writing a book of 200 pages. I didn't know what to do with it. I sent it to *Gunzo* literary magazine to participate in a competition for new writers; I sent it without keeping a copy for myself. I didn't care if I didn't win. Thus the only copy of my first novel disappeared."

Before elaborating on the statement of Haruki Murakami, due to its importance in this context, I have to stop at the point about sending the literary work without keeping a copy for his own. Such deed is considered as madness for writers, but that happened with Mr. Murakami and I know many prominent creators who don't remember where they put a poem they had written, and others who just ignore and look to start something new, wondering what you mean by asking about their last works.

So writing, as we mentioned before, cannot reach the state of holiness as might be believed. Murakami keeps telling his story with writing: "The next spring, I received a call from the editor of *Gunzo* magazine informing me that my novel reached the short list for the award. At that time, I forgot that I participated in such competition. I was busy with many things, even though, my novel was nominated for the award. It was published under the title of *Hear the Wind Sing*. The novel was received with a great amount of admiration. Without realizing what was going on, I found myself among the new generation of Japanese writers. I was surprised along with my family."

No writer is born being sure about his fate (literary career), even if that happens with some writers. It is as if someone says that from childhood he was longing to be an ear, nose, and throat specialist. That cannot be considered a healthy situation, because it hides for the person many horizons where he might produce more and more fruitful and special work. Many writers discovered their talent only suddenly before they largely dominated the arena of their expertise with the originality

146

of their creative products; the examples we mentioned above are proofs of that notion.

The interesting point in the case of Garcia Marquez is that he discovered the way he can write, meaning that he could have been a writer but not as the prestigious Garcia Marquez we know if he adopted other styles, or if he didn't read "The Metamorphosis," which his friend had lent him.

The most interesting part in Murakami's statement is that he felt the desire to write just one novel (receiving well the thing that fell on him from the sky). He didn't have the desire to be a universal novelist. The endeavor for literary fame on the part of a writer or a novelist is legitimate, though it might stop gifted writers from embracing other potential shores of originality and uniqueness in some distant realm in art or in life, too.

It could be obvious from both statements of Garcia Marquez and Murakami that the writer can be surprised by creating something in some way he never imagined, or become talented in a certain literary aspect without prior signs. The most important in this context is that the writer doesn't stop at the first cry of "I can write this way"; writer is believed to go far beyond the usual when he realizes his talent has noticeably and flourishingly blossomed in the gardens of creativity. He would mute his coming surprises: "Oh, I've gone far from my fellow writers," either as an expression of modesty or shyness, or maybe because the writer has become aware that his talents/creativity needs no confirmation from any (literary or cultural) authority.

# Every Writer Can Do Something Else

In *Why We Write*, the American novelist Ann Patchett says: "I swear to God I write because I know nothing rather than writing. Since my childhood I knew that writing is going to be a part of my life. I didn't have any doubt about it. Making such a decision rendered my life meaningful; I put all the eggs in one basket, and here we are, having too many eggs."

Patchett swears that she doesn't know anything but writing. Actually, I don't believe her and I don't want to accuse her of lying, too. She doesn't know that she can do many things along with writing or even without writing if obliged (given certain circumstances of life).

However, Patchett is totally right in the other part of her statement, confirming that writing is going to be something very efficient in her life. The same thing happens with anyone deciding to treat the career he is about to launch accordingly, with only a warning that the concept of "efficient" refers to good productivity leading to success some way or other. Someone may wonder: What should efficiency mean otherwise? The only answer I have is that experience throughout different horizons/ perspectives of professional life, or within the same career, may lead to success in every possible way (though sometimes poor in quantity but with unique/original quality).

If life flows as planned, that would be something rare. We gave an example of someone who was longing since early childhood to be an ear, nose, and throat specialist, and we saw that such case cannot be considered as a healthy phenomenon because it hides for the person many horizons where he might produce more and more fruitful and special work. Of course, it does not mean one has to miss the opportunities granted by life by deciding beforehand to abruptly engage

148

in the labyrinths of human existence/experience. In fact, rocky routes that were unforeseen provide many surprises and joys, apart from the many lessons that come with opting for the tough choices rather than enjoying the simplest shortcuts to "easy" happiness.

Patchett has the ability to do many other things other than writing. In fact, she doesn't have to, and she didn't try to. Not too different from Patchett, we have Kathryn Harrison who states in the same book: "I write because it's the only thing I know and the only thing that makes me worthy of being loved." The difference between the two is that the first feels pride of her success in life through writing and how discovering her talent from the very beginning was useful and vital to her whole career as writer, while the second stresses her feeling of satisfaction only for the fact that writing has made her able to steal into the hearts of her readers.

The American poet Mary Karr states in the same part of the book: "Right now I don't make my living as a writer, but as a university professor instead. I cannot pay the bills from the sales of my books. The myth says that you become rich when you publish a book. Unless that book is welcomed by the masses (of readers), that is totally nonsense. Starting from my fifth year (she means of her career) I always introduce myself as writer and that has nothing to do with payment. I always tell people that I am a poet if they ask me and I keep saying so till now."

Unlike Patchett and Harrison, Karr says: "Before becoming a university teacher of English, I used to run a bar where I worked as a receptionist; I had a funny job in the telecommunication sector. When I stopped drinking, I was a writer for *Harvard Business Review* and I received payments from time to time. I started teaching when I was pregnant with my son, who is 15 years now. I gave lessons at Harvard for $5,000. I taught another course at Tufts University for $3,000. I also gave another course at Emerson College for $1,500. During the five years I had been teaching across different institutions in Boston, I could not live with such revenues. Accordingly, I kept writing essays about marketing for *Harvard Business Review.* This has not developed any of my writing skills or expertise. It just helped me to survive."

It's not important to consider the comparison adopted above. We are not sorting out who is the best in terms of writing approaches or methods, as I am not willing to make you believe that Karr's experience is worthy of consideration as an effective experience, simply because she tried all sorts of work before she decided to devote most of her time (life) to writing.

In short, every writer can do something other than writing, even if that "thing" might be less beautiful/valuable than writing itself. We cannot narrow the circle of creativity to only include one privileged literary genre. We cannot live under the illusion that there is a period of time (an era) for every literary genre to prevail and take over the interest of the audiences. It is illogical to apply the standards governing the arena of "fashion" on the literary and cultural life of people on earth on the basis that every literary trend should respond to the mood of the public/audience eager for the new and the revolutionary so as to quench a thirst for creativity and pleasure. Thus, the trend of the novel is on its way to an end, while another trend is being created somewhere.

Printed in the United States
By Bookmasters